I0639406

Cummings D. Whitcomb, Detroit Steam Navigation Co.

A Lake Tour to Picturesque Mackinac

historical and descriptive - Vol. 1

Cummings D. Whitcomb, Detroit Steam Navigation Co.

A Lake Tour to Picturesque Mackinac
historical and descriptive - Vol. 1

ISBN/EAN: 9783337194758

Printed in Europe, USA, Canada, Australia, Japan

Cover: Foto ©Andreas Hilbeck / pixelio.de

More available books at **www.hansebooks.com**

PRICE 25 CTS.

A Lake Tour

TO

ICTURESQUE

ACKINAC

HISTORICAL AND DESCRIPTIVE.

BY C. D. WHITCOMB.

DETROIT, MICH.:

O. S. GULLEY, BORNMAN & CO., PRINTERS, DETROIT.

1884.

CONTENTS.

ILLUSTRATIONS. Page.

A Lake Tour

to

PICTURESQUE

MACKINAC

VACATION.—Herbert Spencer, in his after dinner speech at the New York banquet said : " We have had somewhat too much of the gospel of work. It is time to preach the gospel of relaxation."

Looking all around us upon this high pressure of American life, we cannot but be convinced of the truth of these words. The editor of the Popular Science Monthly, commenting upon some objections and mis-apprehensions which were raised regarding this speech, says : " Mr. Spencer did not so much condemn strenuous work, in which, indeed, he believes, as the lack of compensating recreations to countervail its mischievous effects." And again, " he has proved the value of recreation as tributary, not only to length of life, but to the perfection of work."

We all know that to repair the exhaustion of nerve and brain, to which people of active intellects are every day subjected, there is no cure but absolute rest. And rest does not merely mean a cessation of work, but a diversion of the mind into new and pleasant channels. This can be most successfully accomplished by a return to Nature, and a complete surrender of one's self to her kindly ministrations.

It seems like idleness to be lolling around at the seashore, at the country farm, or among the mountains, but it is really a repairing and oiling of the human machinery, necessary to the better future accomplishment of work.

The superior man is the one who makes the best use of his natural forces ; the inferior person uses up his vitality, in the shortest space of time.

If, therefore, the brain-workers can find for themselves rest and recreation during the months of July and August, thus renewing the chief forces of life, the whole community, directly or indirectly, gains thereby.

To accomplish this result there are many ways, perhaps none more efficacious than a water trip. As a recent writer has said: " It is truly astonishing how completely we leave carping cares behind as soon as we are fairly afloat. We seem to cut loose from all worries and anxieties, and to be drifting out from the sight and sound of all reminders of the office, study, workshop or household. On the well regulated steamer we are relieved from small responsibilities and annoyances, and in the serene enjoyment of bodily comfort we float lazily and dream, become interested in humanity around us, or the ports into which we occasionally come, and are not expected to be up to the strict requirements of entertaining or being entertained.

In one sense it is Bohemia into which we have entered, and we revel in the freedom, the dolce far niente, the pure, bracing air, and the beauties of sky and sea in which we find ourselves. We watch with a sort of fascination, the leaping spray at the steamer's bow, and fall to noting the ever-changing billows, perhaps remembering Ruskin's remark about the marvellous coloring of a wave. We enter into the little projects for amusement started by other passengers, or perhaps, originate them ourselves, with the zest of a child. In short, on shipboard, whether it be on the ocean or the great lakes, we live a new, novel and fresh life, such as we never at any time experienced upon land.

WHERE SHALL WE GO? To those who enjoy great Nature's work, we would say that Mackinac Island is among the grandest and most romantic. Visitors are voluble with story and legend of every bold cliff and cave and fallen rock around the island shores, and many a pencil, brush and camera are brought to bear on the wonders found.

The invalid comes here because of the wonderful purity of the atmosphere, the climate being especially noted as a sanitarium for hay fever and bronchial affections. Great numbers annually visit this region to escape from or get relief for these maladies, many experiencing an improvement immediately on entering Lake Huron.

The adventurous also comes because the surrounding region offers such endless attractions within easy reach that he cannot fail to find variety if he seeks it. We challenge criticism in saying that no other resort possesses these entertaining features to such great extent, and none is more accessible. Every section of our country sends visitors

6

Mackinac Island—From the decks of Detroit and Cleveland Steam Navigation Co.'s Steamers.

annually to this region, and their testimony will substantiate our claims. Gamey fish in great variety lurk in all the numerous inland lakes and rivers, with which the wonderful State of Michigan abounds, while its forests which are the hiding places of more than the usual varieties of furred and feathered creatures, afford facilities for fine sport.

MACKINAC ISLAND is reached by the Detroit and Cleveland Steam Navigation Company, by their pleasant route through the lakes, with a splendid line of palatial side-wheel iron steamers, the largest, swiftest and most luxurious of any on fresh waters, the excellence and completeness of whose service caused the writer to select their line as the connecting link by water to this famed island resort and sanitarium. The few landings made enroute are just sufficient to interest without being tedious.

During the summer months their steamers stop at the Island, both going and returning, which gives those who wish to return on the same trip, from four to six hours in which to view the curiosities and the wonders of the place, carriages being always on hand on arrival ; or, by remaining until the next steamer, over thirty-six hours is given. Return tickets are good by either steamer on any trip during the season. The round trip occupies but four and one-half days from Cleveland. By stopping over at the Island from one steamer to another you would be gone six and one-half days, so that your stay can be lengthened by about two days, as best suits your convenience.

Passengers taking this company's steamers, City of Detroit and Northwest, which leave Cleveland every week day at 20.30 o'clock, can time it to make close connections at Detroit with the steamers City of Mackinac or City of Cleveland, which leave Detroit every Wednesday and Friday morning at 10 o'clock, and Monday and Saturday nights at 22 o'clock for Mackinac. The quickest trip and closest connection from Cleveland is made by taking the company's steamer City of Detroit Tuesday or Thursday evening.

WHAT WILL IT COST ? This depends somewhat on circumstances. Tickets covering transportation only are very cheap, being only $4.50 one way, or $7.00 for round trip from Cleveland; (half fare for children between five and twelve years of age,)can be procured from any railroad ticket agent. Those who prefer to bring a well filled lunch basket, and do not care for a place to sleep, need not incur any additional expense, as they can occupy a comfortable chair in one of the elegant saloons in the forward part of the steamer. Should you prefer meals, one or more can be had at 50 cents each. The same

The Viaduct, Cleveland, O.

price is charged for children over three years old; under that age, 25 cents, and they can be brought to the first table.

The running time from Cleveland to Mackinac includes five meals, which at 50 cents each would amount to $2.50 each way. The only additional expense is for a berth, which can be had for $2.00 for an upper berth of single width, or $3.00 for a lower berth of double width. Put the items together, say for

	Single Trip.	Round Trip.
Transportation	$ 4.50..	$ 7.00
5 meals at 50 cents each	2.50..	5.00
An upper berth	2.00..	4.00
Total with upper berth	$9.00..	$16 00
Extra for a lower berth	1.00 .	2.00
Total with lower berth	..$10.00..	$18.00
Or for two persons in one room ($9 and $10)	19 00 ..	34.00 or $17 each.
For three persons in one room, add the transportation and meals only for the extra person	7.00..	12.00
Total cost for three persons, occupying but one room, from Cleveland to Mackinac, $26.00	$46 00	(or $15.34) each.

All berths are in state rooms, and each room has two berths and will accommodate two or three persons. Meals and berths are arranged for, exclusively by the company. The demand for sleeping accommodations during the tourists' season is such that each state room on the steamers from Detroit to Mackinac must accommodate at least two persons at the price named. Those wishing to occupy a room alone, however, can make special arrangements at Cleveland with Mr. T. F. Newman, agent, at company's wharf.

For the benefit of those who find it difficult to realize the comparative cheapness of this delightful trip by water, we would call attention to the 956 miles in the round trip, occupying 4½ days costing only $16.00 to $18.00, or about $3.75 per day. How, and where, can you go and compass so much enjoyment and solid comfort by the way. Should you be inclined to go by rail, remember the rates they quote do not provide for meals, neither do they include sleeping accommodations. If you reach Mackinac sooner by that means, a fair comparison would include meals and sleeping car fare on the way, together with hotel bills incurred until the steamer gets there, which three items alone

Lake View Park, Cleveland, O.

will be found to cover the entire cost by water, and the rail fare has not
yet been considered, which for the same number of miles would be
cheap at $20, or, say $36 in all, or twice as much as by water. " I have
never taken this view of the facts, its a good one," is the usual answer
when the subject of a trip to Mackinac is discussed from this stand
point.

Again, it is presumed that a summer trip is planned to get all the
pleasure and fresh air possible. By rail, it is hot and dusty, and you
are cramped for room, and what little strength you started with would
most likely be used up by the round trip ; especially would this be the
case with ladies and children. One way by steamer even would be
better than none at all. The most attractive and varied scenery would
be found on a water trip, with ample time for a good look at every
interesting object. In fact all that can be said in favor of rail is the
quick arrival, which is certainly the least object on a trip for pleasure.
rest and recreation. You leave home for a vacation. Why ? Naturally
to reverse the excitement of business cares, the bustle, hurry and rushing about. Such relief is fully obtained, only by taking a water trip.
Try it once

On entering Cleveland, the Transfer Co., whose employees attend
all trains will take charge of your baggage and transfer you (without
cost, if you are provided with through tickets having a transfer coupon
attached) to the steamer lying at the company's wharf, 23 River street,
where meals can be had at regular hours for 50 cents, or, if late, a lunch
at 25 cents. Between Cleveland and Detroit the fare is only $2.25 for
transportation, which is one-half of rail fare. Berths are all in state
rooms (two in each room) and are graded in price according to location,
those forward and aft are $1.00 for an upper berth of single width, and
$1.50 for a lower berth of double width, the cheapest rooms having
three berths are amidships ; the upper is 50 cents, the lower 75 cents.
Among the advanced steps taken by this company, is that of not
including berths in their ticket fares, which happily disposes of the
vexatious question how to best take care of their patrons comfortably.
Now, very many do without berths, and by the graded prices the best
is practically reserved for those who want them most, and the accommodations are seldom over-taxed. The state rooms are furnished with
wire and hair mattrasses, sheets are long and clean, blankets are of the
Pullman style, and as many as are needed for your comfort. The local
travel between these two cities is largely composed of commercial
travelers, who transact their business in either city during the day time,
and take advantage of the quiet rest at night en-route.

13

Harbor at Cleveland, O.—Mouth of Cuyahoga River.

CLEVELAND, at the mouth of Cuyahoga river, on the southern shore of Lake Erie is situated on a plain from eighty to one hundred feet above the lake, and has a population of 210,000. Its distance from Detroit is one hundred and ten miles by water, and one hundred and seventy-two by rail. The city was founded in 1796, by Gen. Moses Cleaveland. He entered the river in charge of a party sent by the Connecticut Land Company to survey their property on the western Reserve, which resulted in the laying out of a small portion of land, on which was erected a store-house and several rude cabins, which comprised the town. Edward Paine, of New York State, is said to have been the first to transact business at this point. The second year the population was increased by several families, among whom was Miss Chloe Inches, the first young lady resident of the valley. Prospects of its becoming a large city soon became evident. The mouth of the river was originally the only harbor, and frequently became so choked with sand as to form a dry crossing. Very few vessels attempted to enter the river, cargoes being landed in lighters; yet as early as 1805 it was of sufficient importance to make it a port of entry. No successful attempt at improvement was made until 1826, when the government made an appropriation to cut a new channel, build piers and remove obstructions.

Sept. 1st, 1818, Walk-in-the-Water, the first steamer to sail on the lakes entered the port, en-route, Buffalo to Detroit. Great excitement prevailed, and round after round of artillery announced her arrival and departure. In 1819, Josiah Barber built a log cabin, and became the first settler on the west side. In 1831, the Buffalo Company purchased a farm there, dotting the low land at the mouth of the river with warehouses, and the adjacent bluffs with stores, dwellings and hotels, thus starting the foundation of a town which bid fair to rival the settlement on the east side. Further efforts obtained a city charter, under the name of Ohio City. This aroused the slumbering jealousies of the east siders, and finally culminated in 1837 in what was known as "The Battle of the Bridge." This bridge which connected what is now Cleveland

14

with Brooklyn was built in 1835, by J. S. Clark, who dedicated it to public use when finished. Both cities had received their charters, known as Ohio City on the west and Cleveland on the east, and each claimed jurisdiction over the bridge. Resolutions and treaties availing nothing, each city sent armed men to take possession. A field piece was so placed as to sweep the bridge from the east, and war began. Weapons and missiles of all kinds were freely used, several persons were badly wounded, and the bridge considerably damaged before the sheriff and city marshal succeeding in quelling the riot, and transferring the question of ownership to the courts.

At High Bridge Glens - Cuyahoga Falls—The Niagara of Ohio.

In 1855, Ohio City was annexed to Cleveland, which is now one of the wealthiest and most prosperous cities of the west. Its manufacturing advantages attracts capital from all parts of the country. Traffic in iron and copper ores, lumber, oil and coal, have developed into gigantic proportions, making this the principal port on lake Erie.

In 1827 Cleveland was connected with Akron by a canal, which ran through important coal fields.

There was no demand for coal in Cleveland at this time, and the story of the first load is somewhat interesting, considering the present vast importance of the trade. Henry Newberry, who owned valuable coal land, fancied he saw an opening for extensive trade in the article, and sent a few tons to the city for trial. A wagon load was carted around all day, its quality and value as fuel presented, but with small encouragement, as wood was plentiful, and a feeling of distrust existed as to whether the stony substance would serve for fuel at all. Philo Scoville, proprietor of the Franklin House, finally purchased a small quantity at two dollars per ton, placed grates in the house, gave the coal a trial, and a wide spread reputation for the valuable article was thus established. The amount now consumed in Cleveland is enormous. and exportations exceed those of any other lake port. The traffic in iron ore is extensive, nearly the entire product of the Lake Superior region centers here for distribution in all directions, the mines being principally owned and controlled by Cleveland capitalists.

The rapid improvements of the city are worthy of special note. The breakwater constructed by the government is one mile long, encloses two hundred acres of still water, forms a harbor of refuge, and furnishes extensive dockage facilities.

The viaduct, an immense structure, whose length is 3211 feet. spans the valley of the Cuyahoga, and connects the east and west sides. From Superior street to the draw, the construction is principally iron trestle work. The draw alone is 362 feet. The west side consists of ten stone arches, eight being 83, and two 97½ feet span. The length of road bed thus supported is 1,382 feet, at an elevation of 54 feet. Cost, $2,150,000. The N. Y., C. & St. L. R. R. viaduct is another monument of engineering skill. It is constructed wholly of iron, with stone abutments. Total length, 3,050 feet; elevation, 68 feet, and crosses the Cuyahoga valley diagonally, but a short distance south of the city viaduct. The entire business portion of the city is lighted by electricity, from the top of huge iron masts, ranging in height from 200 to 260 feet.

The manufacturing industries are chiefly located in the valley, leaving much of the higher lands for residences, thus causing strangers to wonder where the business necessary to support so many inhabitants is carried on. Cleveland is sometimes called " Forest City," on account of the beautiful lawns and broad, shady avenues which meet the eye in all directions. Visitors should not neglect the opportunity of a drive

16

on the far-famed Euclid avenue, the finest residence street in the world.

At High Bridge Glens—Cuyahoga Falls—The Niagara of Ohio.

There are many fine cemeteries and public and private parks. From Lake View park a fine view of the shipping is obtained. It is a famous promenade, and a most attractive and picturesque spot. Thousands visit its mossy banks on summer evenings, to delight in the cool breezes and watch the setting sun sink into the broad bosom of the lake. These sunsets, beautiful beyond description, are visible only where land and water hold a similar geographical relation. Wade park, containing one hundred acres, has many natural advantages. It was donated to the city by Hon. J. H. Wade, who lavished large sums, and displayed exquisite taste in beautifying it. This park lies four miles from the city hall, on the Euclid avenue and Prospect street railway.

17

Three quarters of a mile east of this park, is Lake View cemetery, an extensive enclosure, combining all the advantages of Nature and art. It contains many grand monuments and costly tombs. Here lies the remains of the illustrious Garfield, guarded by U. S. troops, and on an eminence close by, is carefully preserved the funeral car which bore the martyred President to his final resting place.

Every week-day, at 20.30 o'clock, the steamer City of Detroit, or Northwest, leaves the wharf, 23 River street. Fifteen minutes are consumed in getting out of the river. A bright light, which is noticed on the port bow, is placed on a crib, built as a protection to the lake tunnel, through which Cleveland receives its water supply. The crib is built of 12 inch white pine timbers, 61 feet high, pentagonal in form, each side measuring 54 feet. The sides of the inner wall form well holes, each measuring 19 feet. From the outer to the inner wall is 24 feet, with a third wall midway between the two. The whole is covered with 2 inch oak plank, and at the water line with boiler plate half an inch thick, and five feet deep, as a protection to the timber from the action of ice. The space between the outer and inner walls is filled with stone, a large quantity of which is also piled around the outside. The lake tunnel is 1¼ miles long, its diameter over five feet. Depth of lake shaft, 90 feet; shore shaft, 67 feet below the water; diameter of each, 8 feet.

Lake Erie washes the shores of New York, Pennsylvania, Ohio, Michigan and Canada; it is 250 miles long by 40 to 60 wide; greatest depth, 204 feet. Its surface is 565 feet above Hudson river at Albany, and 330 above Lake Ontario. The coast line of the great lakes and shores of the St. Lawrence river are 3,206 miles on the American side, and 2,451 on the Canadian side, a total of 5,657 miles, or nearly a quarter of the circumference of the earth.

For many who will be interested in the power which drives the steamer, a good view of the engine is had through the large plate glass in the main saloon The smooth, easy motion of this heavy mass of machinery excites wonder and astonishment. Every neat housekeeper will find her efforts equalled by the bright, clean appearance of every utensil and piece of machinery in the engine room, and the engineer on duty will cheerfully explain.

The two columns are steam pipes. The one on the left contains steam, as it comes direct from the boiler, and is held there under full pressure by valves in the two steam chests. one above and one below, until wanted by the cylinder, a large, round body just behind the steam chests, in which a piston works up and down.

18

The long rod on the left opens the upper valve, admitting steam to the cylinder, which forces the piston down, while the short rod opens the lower valve, admitting steam under the piston, which forces it up. This up and down working of the piston moves all the machinery. Motion is first given by opening the valves by hand a few times after which an eccentric arm from the main shaft does the work, automatically At every full stroke of the piston the paddle wheels turn half round. The piston is connected by rods to one end of the walking

Light House, Cleveland, O.

beam, the other end of which is connected by rods with a crank on the main shaft, running across the steamer. With each end of the shaft a paddle wheel is connected.

The rods on the right open the valves from the cylinder, just as the piston finishes the stroke, and the steam which was but a moment

19

before let in from the left column to move the piston, now rushes out into the right hand column, to give the piston a clear space to work back again as soon as steam is let in on the other side to drive it. Motion is thus obtained by steam forcing the piston down from the top, then up from the bottom. Each time the piston moves the length of the cylinder, the steam which moved it must be gotten out of the way before it can move back again.

Under the right hand column is the condenser, containing a spray of cold water, which strikes the steam as it enters, condensing it instantly ; thus converting what was a large volume of steam into a very small quantity of water. The sudden collapsing of this great bulk of steam in an air tight column, creates a vacuum in the cylinder which exhausted the steam, which means there is nothing in the cylinder to obstruct the passage of the piston, not even air. A perfect vacuum is as good as carrying fifteen pounds of extra steam in the boilers.

The crank room, with its complicated machinery is just beyond, and the boiler room is in the hold of the steamer, which can be seen from the main deck. There the fireman will be found busily shovelling coal into the furnaces. This room is lined on all sides with boiler plate, and is a complete water tight compartment. Stop for one moment and contemplate the perfect harmony with which this great mass, made up of little parts, moves, obedient to the will of one mind.

From the end of the piers our steamer heads W. x N. $\frac{1}{4}$ N. for $3\frac{1}{2}$ hours to Point Pelee Light, sometimes called the Dummy, which is fifty miles from Cleveland and sixty from Detroit. This takes us across the open lake.

Point Pelee is a headland on the Canadian shore, which projects for several miles into the lake at the entrance to Pigeon Bay, and with the many islands in the vicinity, form the most picturesque scenery on Lake Erie. W. x N. course for twenty-five minutes brings us to Point Pelee Island Light. This island belongs to Canada, is seven miles long, and two and a half wide, abounds in red cedar and fine limestone, and contains a few inhabitants. Several small islands lie to the south, called the East Middle and West Sister and Hen and Chickens. Farther on are the North, Middle and South Bass; on the west side of the latter lies the secure harbor of Put-in-Bay, celebrated as the rendezvous of Commodore Perry's flotilla, before and after the glorious naval victory over the British fleet September 10th, 1813, and is the very spot from which was sent the famous dispatch: "We have met the enemy, and they are ours."

Kelley's Island is the largest and most important of the group, and is famous for its grape culture and native wines. These islands are

20

reached from Detroit by steamers, which leave every morning except Sundays. From Point Pelee Island we run across Pigeon Bay on a W. ½ N. course for one hour and ten minutes, to Colchester light ship, located but three miles out from Colchester, Canada. One hour more on the same course brings us to Bar Point light ship, near the entrance to

Scene in Public Square, Cleveland, O.

Detroit river. If you care to rise at this hour—about four—you will be well repaid by the early morning trip up the river. An order left with the cabin watchman to call you if the morning is clear will receive attention.

Father Hennepin, who passed up the river in early days enthusiastically wrote: "The islands are the finest in the world; the strait is finer than Niagara; the banks are vast meadows, and the prospect terminates

21

with some hills crowned with vineyards, fruit bearing trees, groves and forests so well disposed that one would think Nature alone could not have made, without the help of art, so charming a prospect." Civilization has somewhat marred its freshness, but the strait still affords some of the loveliest river scenery in America.

There are fifteen islands between Bar Point and Detroit, and a zig-zag course is taken to clear them. Leaving Bar Point light ship, we round Bar Point and into the river by courses N. W. x N. $\frac{1}{2}$ N. for six minutes, N. x W. $\frac{1}{4}$ W. five minutes, and N. $\frac{3}{4}$ E. four and one half minutes. The river is twenty-seven miles long, and one half to three miles wide, with a current of three miles per hour. N. x E. $\frac{3}{4}$ E. course for eleven minutes brings us to Bois Blanc Island light, then N. $\frac{1}{2}$ W. for four minutes to abreast of Amherstburg, Canada, N. x W. $\frac{1}{4}$ W. three minutes to head of Bois Blanc Island, N. x E. five minutes to the Lime Kiln crossing.

The water at this point is shallow and the current swift, owing to a ledge of rocks which obstruct the channel. This spot is the key to the depth of water which grain and ore vessels can draw, and seriously affects the entire commerce of the lakes. A violent wind blowing down the river forces the water out of Lake Erie so rapidly as to lower it at this crossing, and heavily laden freight vessels are often obliged to lay over until the wind shifts or dies away, when the water resumes its usual depth. The government has expended a large amount of money and labor in removing the obstructions, but not enough of either at one time to afford immediate relief to the vast interests that suffer. The loss sustained by damages to craft striking the bottom, lightering of cargoes and delay, is each year more than sufficient to perfect the improvements. N W. x N. $\frac{3}{4}$ N. from the crossing for nineteen minutes, brings us to the head of Grosse Isle, then N. $\frac{3}{4}$ E. five minutes, Mamma Judy light, N. $\frac{1}{2}$ W., five minutes abreast of Wyandotte, N. $\frac{1}{2}$ E. five minutes, abreast of Grassy Island light; N. $\frac{3}{4}$ W. six minutes, to a point on Fighting Island; N. E. x N. $\frac{1}{8}$ N. twenty-three minutes, Sandwich Mineral Springs, Canada; N. E. $\frac{1}{2}$ N. seven minutes, to Sandwich Point, and a sharp turn to N. E. $\frac{1}{2}$ E. brings the city into full view. On the left is Fort Wayne, which is garrisoned and mounted with heavy ordnance; on the right is Sandwich, Canada, and further on Windsor.

Eight minutes lands us at the Michigan Central railroad depot, where passengers for the interior leave the steamer. The Detroit Omnibus Line here offer every facility in the way of omnibuses, baggage wagons, carriages and coupes. Mackinac passengers can have breakfast on this steamer if they wish.

After discharging what is destined for this wharf, the steamer pro-
ceeds to the Company's Wayne street wharf, where on Wednesday and
Friday mornings the steamer City of Mackinac or City of Cleveland
will be found nearly ready to sail. Mondays and Saturdays they do not

Gordon Park, Cleveland, O.

leave until night, which gives an excellent opportunity to view the
beauties of Detroit. Steamers City of Detroit and Northwest leave
Detroit for Cleveland every week day at 22 o'clock.

 **DETROIT,** with a population of 140,-000, is the oldest city of the west, and the metropolis of the Peninsula State. It was from the first an important trading post, and as larger interests developed, became a city of excellent material prophecies; now in the full flush of prosperity it reaches out its iron arms to grasp that commercial supremacy which it will attain with all the absolute certainty with which cause is followed by effect. More than to any other source save its fine location, the city owes its steady and solid advancement to its spirited, whole souled mercantile class, by whose influence and money the majority of Michigan railroads have been built.

The prospective importance of Detroit was first pointed out by the Jesuit missionaries, whose sagacity has been similarly exemplified in selecting the sites of numerous other cities, St. Louis, New Orleans, Montreal, etc.

To the gallant and enterprising De La Motte Cadillac, belongs the honor of founding Detroit, in 1701. The early settlers who followed in his train found upon the shores of the noble river, homes more attractive than any their wildest dreams had pictured.

Fort Ponchartrain was here erected, and the small military garrison, a few fur traders and Jesuit missionaries made up the population. For about a century but little progress was perceptible in growth and population. The interior of the state remained an unbroken wilderness, and the city was dependent for business on its Indian trade alone.

The little settlement was often visited by the fortunes of ' grim visaged war,' and at one time became an important point in the momentous struggle between England and France for a dominating power in the affairs of the new world. No less than five times was there a change in the national emblem, floating over the place. The silver lilies flaunted over the infant fortress, to be succeeded by the cross of St. George, which was supplanted by the stars and stripes, these giving away for a short season to the red cross, which was again finally lowered to the lasting supremacy of the American flag. Once was it captured, once burnt to the ground, and it was the scene of 50 pitched battles and twelve massacres.

24

In 1712, Cadillac closed his administration of affairs amid a sea of troubles, the most vital of which was the question of " liquor traffic,' against which the Jesuit fathers had set their faces. It will thus be seen that the subject which is now so powerfully agitating the public mind is not altogether so new and fresh as might at first be supposed since it was an important bone of contention nearly two hundred years ago.

Wade Park, Cleveland, O.

In 1763, Detroit, with the other French possessions in the north, passed into the hands of the British. This was immediately followed by the famous Pontiac conspiracy by which the Indians, under the leadership of this able chief sought to exterminate the white race throughout the northwest. The projected massacre was defeated at this point by a Chippewa girl's betrayal of the scheme to Major Gladwyn, commander of the post, who was thus put on his guard. A siege of eleven months followed, the fort holding out nobly against the enraged savages.

In 1796, under the supplementary treaty of peace with Great Britain, Detroit was turned over to the United States.

But it must not be supposed that the young " City of the Straits " was the theatre of nothing but war and bloodshed Ah! no Romance

25

and song and love, were as much a part of its life as these sterner realities of history. Past its green shores, down the beautiful river floated the merry carol of the voyageur, and many a birch bark canoe with its cargo of furs swung out into the stream to the melody of these quaint old canzonets. Says Constance Fennimore Woolson, in Appleton's Journal : '' The little river settlement was a favorite post of these hardy hunters, a race by themselves—looking at this distance very romantic, with their roving lives, their love for frolicing and dancing, and their wild love songs, sung as the loaded bateaux moved out into the current of the broad river. Some of these melodies still preserve a place in American music; they have a character of their own, too quick for the slow Englishman, too gay for the sober American, essentially French in every note and word.''

Wine was abundant, being made from the wild grapes which grew in profusion on the shore, and that the settlers had imported with them the social manners of la belle France sufficiently to know how to use it, is evinced by the following passage from an old note book of 1778: '' The citizens all lived as one family, had Detroit assemblies once a week, where the ladies never went without being in their silks; dining parties were frequent, and they drank their wine freely.''

In 1778 the old fort had been removed, the village enlarged, and a new fort erected on the high ground further back from the river. This was named Fort LeNoult, and occupied a space now bounded by Lafayette avenue, Congress street, a line a little east of · Shelby street, and one west of Wayne street. Heavy stockades extended from either side of the fort to the river, forming a rude triangle, of which the river was the base. Within this stockade was comprised the village, with a population of sixty families. The streets were narrow, the widest being but twenty feet, and the houses were low and mainly of wood. That in 1805 a fire should break out and sweep away the entire village was therefore not surprising. But a single house remained standing.

Two years later Congress authorized the laying out of a city on a much more liberal scale, and made a grant of 10,000 acres of land to aid in defraying the cost of the necessary improvements. The authorship of the plan of the new city is attributed to Judge Woodward, who was a man of exceedingly fanciful tastes, as was evinced by his design.

There were to be several open squares, with broad avenues radiating from them, like the spokes of a wheel. The streets were to be of unusual width, and access from one part of the city to another was exceedingly convenient; but the objection was the amount of land wasted and the angular shape of a great proportion of the lots; consequently

River Bank, near the St. Clair Mineral Springs.

at a later period the Woodward plan was abandoned, only a small portion of which is still retained, the rectangular system being substituted. Between the two plans and the freedom which was accorded to every property holder to lay out streets and subdivide his property after his own taste, Detroit is to-day perhaps as labyrinthian a city as any in the west.

In 1812, war broke out with Great Britain, and on the 16th of August following, General Hull, who was in command, surrendered the fort and city to General Brock, without any attempt to maintain a defense. The British remained in possession for more than a year, when, as a result of the American victory at the battle of the Thames, it was recovered by the United States. The name of the fort was now changed to Shelby. At this time the population was less than one thousand, and its growth for a long time continued very slow.

In 1831, when the population had reached two thousand, the first real step was taken towards opening up the interior and making it tributary to the city, in the commencement of the construction of what is now the Michigan Central Railroad. The work progressed slowly, and it was not until February, 1838 that any part of the line was opened for traffic.

In 1836, and again in 1840 and 1848, disastrous fires swept away large portions of the city. In 1827 the fort was abandoned by the government, and being made over to the city was demolished, the earth forming its embankments being carted down to the river and dumped into the shallow water. The shore line was thus extended out into the river, in some places an entire block.

In 1847 the city lost its prestige as capital of the State, the legislative seat being removed to Lansing. In 1854 it secured direct communication with the east by the opening of the Great Western Railway, of Canada, and four years later a competing line in the completion of the Grand Trunk.

In 1860, though occupying no less an area than at present, it was much more sparsely settled. The larger part of the Cass farm was still what its name indicates, and fields abutted on Woodward avenue, within the two mile radius. Only a few leading thoroughfares were paved. There were neither street railways nor omnibus lines, and old fashioned drays did all the hauling. No public street lamps were to be found, except in the central part, and where the city hall now stands, was a group of old wooden rookeries, once the depot buildings of the M.C.R.R. The parks were uncared for, and overgrown with grass and weeds. One ferry boat, the Gem, accommodated all the traffic between Detroit and Windsor. There was no police force, no house of correction, and only a black hole for a jail. Since then the progress has been very rapid,

28

Front Street, near the St. Clair Mineral Springs.

and large tracts which were at that time open commons, are now densely covered with houses. The wholesale trade and manufacturing interests have nearly absorbed the lower part of the city near the river, and the retail traffic spreads out continuously towards the extreme limits on every avenue leading from the central square, called Campus Martius, invading the haunts of the former aristocratic residents, who are fast seeking other locations, and building up the vacant spots on the outskirts with a class of elegant homes unsurpassed elsewhere.

Detroit covers an area some six miles in length, on the river, by a depth of two and a half miles, and although located near the extreme southwest corner of the State, is the chief city and commercial metropolis of Michigan. It is on the right bank of the river, (or, more properly, a strait, Detroit being the French term for strait,) is seven miles below lake St. Clair, and twenty miles above lake Erie. Through this strait passes the vast tonnage of the great lakes, which in volume exceeds the entire foreign commerce of the country. The river here is $\frac{3}{4}$ of a mile wide, and is everywhere navigable by the largest craft, affording the city a magnificient water front miles in extent. This fine location at the only point between lakes Erie and St. Clair, suitable for a large harbor, constituted the place from earliest times an important point in the traffic of this region, and has undoubtedly been the key to its steady and genuine advancement, also affording a sure guarantee of its future substantial progress

Having ample ground, the dwellings are not crowded together in solid blocks, but are mostly detached, with plenty of intervening space. This, with the breadth of the streets and the prevalence of shade trees, gives the place more of a village than a city air, and contributes much to its attractiveness as a place of residence. As a healthful city it is without a peer.

Churches are very numerous in proportion to the population. The school system is admirable, bearing favorable comparison with that of any other city. Society, too, from the less frequent changes that obtain here, as compared with other western cities, is more settled, refined and truly polite. Thus, as a place of residence it is unsurpassed by any place west of Boston. Indeed, while the business activity and stir of Chicago is lacking, it resembles Boston not a little in its social and literary atmosphere.

The Germans claim a third of the population, and there is still considerable of the old original French element left. In the days of pro-slavery, this city was noted for being the headquarters of the underground railway, and there is naturally a large population of the colored

St. Clair Mineral Springs Driving Park.

race, while Hollanders, Poles, Swedes, Norwegians, Swiss, Italians, etc., represent the European nationalities in considerable numbers; but this foreign element is eminently industrious, thrifty and orderly. In general each family owns its homestead. The savings banks are well patronized, and vagrancy and pauperism are perhaps as little prevalent here as in any city of the same size in the United States.

Detroit is a wealthy city. Most of the business operations of its citizens are based on real capital, owned by the parties using it, and not borrowed elsewhere. This is undoubtedly the result of the extreme conservatism which borders a little on lack of enterprise, or which at least shuns speculation. This conservatism, for which the city has been noted, has limited her growth to a strictly healthy and natural one. It has prevented over trading in any department of business; and thus we find an almost entire absence of inflation. Real estate is relatively cheap, and few branches of business are overdone. This condition of things renders the city a peculiarly inviting field for men of enterprise and capital to locate in. Competition has not dried up the vital sources of wealth, and its financial credit is unimpeachable.

Notwithstanding the admirable condition of the public works, the debt is small. Taxes are light. For a number of years past the financial affairs of the city have been managed with great wisdom and fidelity, and there are few municipal wants unprovided for. The water supply is ample and placed beyond a contingency of failure, extensive pumping works being located a few miles above the city.

Detroit is essentially a manufacturing city, possessing from its easy water communication and its proximity to the inexhaustible mines and forests of the State, peculiar advantages. There can be no doubt that the time is coming when the banks of the strait will be lined with mills and factories that will render it the Birmingham of the northwest.

The site of the city has a gradual rise from the river until an elevation of fifty feet is reached in the northern limits. This elevation is so gradual as to almost escape the notice of visitors. It affords every opportunity for perfect drainage, and the city enjoys the reputation of having the cleanest and most wholesome of streets. Street car lines give cheap transportation to all parts, and the Detroit omnibus line, an enterprising company, furnishes prompt and satisfactory services with omnibuses, baggage wagons, coaches and coupes.

To the visitor the city soon becomes most enchanting as a place of quiet, rest and enjoyment. It is essentially a residence town; a great number of wealthy people have sought it as a place for their homes, and their fine residences and spacious grounds are to be found in all directions.

U

BAY

Buffalo Riv.

Standish

Mt. Saginaw

materially inci

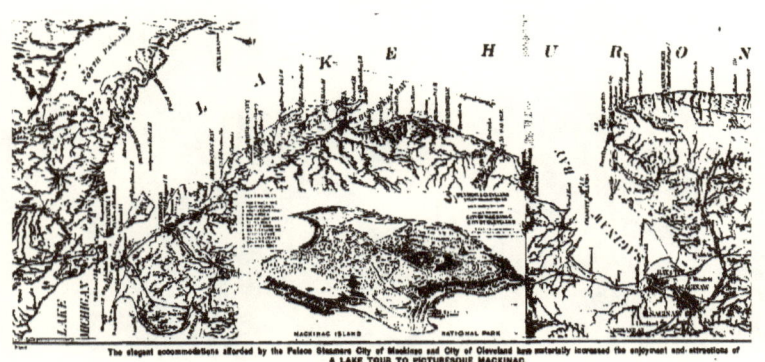

The elegant accommodations afforded by the Palace Steamers City of Mackinac and City of Cleveland have materially increased the enjoyment and attractions of
A LAKE TOUR TO PICTURESQUE MACKINAC.

View of Detroit Harbor from Windsor, Canada, opposite Detroit and Cleveland Steam Navigation Co.'s Wharf.

Detroit is one of the most complete and desirable of summer resorts in the world, possessing all the requirements of a popular watering place, together with all the advantages and luxuries of a city home. The river is the pride of its residents, and the surprise and delight of tourists, who pronounce it one of the most beautiful streams in the world. It has a current of three miles an hour, and has never been known to rise more than seventeen inches above its regular level.

In the channel opposite the upper portion of the city is Belle Isle park, containing about 700 acres. It was purchased by the city for $200,000, and is a favorite resort, easily reached in the summer by a service of fine ferry steamers, every twenty minutes. There are seventeen other islands in the river, many of which are attractive for excursion parties and summer residences, with frequent communication with the city by steamers. Names and location of these islands are found by referring to the bird's eye view.

Detroit challenges comparison as being the handsomest city in the Union, a fact admitted by all, who, by reason of extended travel and close observation are best fitted to judge. In addition to her acquired beauties, she is extravagantly favored by Nature. The broad river is easily reached from almost any part of the city, giving in summer immediate escape from heat, dust and noise, which great luxury is within the power of all.

Ten cents gives you a ride back and forth across the river all the afternoon, 50 cents takes you through lake St. Clair to Star Island, or down the river to Put-in-Bay, or $1.00 to Oakland House, St. Clair Mineral Springs, and return. In fact there are a dozen or more popular, healthful and beautiful resorts within from one to three hours' ride from Detroit, by steamer, and at a nominal cost. No time need be wasted, and no one need be at a loss for something to do, or somewhere to go. Detroit is the center of all these attractions, and it is not an unusual sight during the pleasant days of summer to witness the arrival of five thousand strangers in the city in a single day, from the interior towns within a radius of one hundred and fifty miles.

The resorts of most cities are but few, and from four to twenty-four hours away, while here you can return at a seasonable hour the same evening. Truly it would seem that those seeking for a place in which to pass the summer as comfortably as possible, with a desire to see and enjoy, would not fail to select Detroit in preference to all others, and the ever increasing number of visitors and transient residents from the east, and especially from the south, is conclusive evidence that the above facts are rapidly being appreciated.

34

By Steamers, from Cleveland and Detroit.

Of the large, elegant steamers of the Detroit and Cleveland Steam Navigation Company's fleet, the City of Detroit and Northwest leave Detroit every evening, except Sundays, at 22 o'clock, landing you in Cleveland at 5.30 o'clock the following morning, in season for the early trains for the east or south.

This night line by water between two such important commercial cities as Cleveland and Detroit is a boon to the commercial traveler who works by day and travels by night, anxious to make every hour tell to advantage, and being usually confined to the hot, dusty, rumbling rail car,

Ship Building on Pine River, near St. Clair Mineral Springs.

as the only method of getting about, naturally avails himself of this agreeable change, to a charming quiet, and a full night's rest. The breath of fresh air, in the cool breeze made by the speed of the steamer is refreshing in itself, especially if the day has been sultry on shore. The delightful two hours' run down the river on moonlight nights allures many from their couches.

A trip of thirty hours by the City of Mackinac Wednesday mornings at 10 o'clock, and Saturday nights at 22 o'clock, or the City of Cleveland Monday nights at 22 o'clock, and Friday mornings at 10 o'clock brings you to the great historic summer resort and sanitarium, Mackinac Island. Their time-table shows distances, and the running time between, and hours of departure from way ports.

35

Summer Resorts of
LAKES HURON, MICHIGAN AND SUPERIOR,
Via MACKINAC ISLAND.

| STATIONS. | RATES. | | | | ROUTE |
| | FROM CLEVELAND. | | FROM DETROIT. | | From Mackinac Is'd. |
	Single.	Round.	Single.	Round.	
Ashland........Wis.	$20.50	$37.00	$19.00	$35.00	L. M. & L. S. T. Co.
Bayfield....... "	20.50	37.00	19.00	35.00	L. M. & L. S. T. Co.
Charlevoix....Mich.	6.50	10.00	5.00	8.00	Hannah, Lay & Co.
Chicago.........Ill.	11.50	20.00	10.00	18.00	L.M.Line. L.M.&L.S T.Co.
Crooked Lake,Mich.	6.25	10.00	4.75	8.00	Inland Nav. Co.
Duluth.......Minn.	20.50	37.00	19.00	35.00	L. M. & L. S. T. Co.
Elk Rapids,...Mich.	7.50	12.25	6.00	10.25	Hannah, Lay & Co.
Escanaba..... "	11.50	20.50	10.00	18.50	Smith & Adams.
Frankfort..... "	9.00	16.00	7.50	14.00	N. M. Line.
Green Bay.....Wis.	13.00	23.50	11.50	21.50	Smith & Adams.
Hancock.....Mich.	16.50	27.00	15.00	25.00	L. M. & L. S. T. Co.
" "	14.50	25.80	13.00	23.80	D., M. & M. R. R.
Harbor Springs, "	6.00	9.50	4.50	7.50	N.M.L'e.H.L.&.Co.
Houghton.... "	16.50	27.00	15.00	25.00	L. M. & L. S. T. Co.
" .... "	14.25	25.30	12.75	23.30	D., M. & M. R. R.
Indian River, "	5.00	8.00	3.50	6.00	Inland Nav. Co.
L'Anse....... "	16.50	27.00	15.00	25.00	L. M. & L. S. T. Co.
" .... "	13.00	22.80	11.50	20.80	D., M. & M. R. R.
Leland...... "	8.00	14.00	6.50	12.00	N. M. Line.
Mackinac Is'd, "	Tourist.	11.35		9.35	M.C.Ry M'k. to D't.
Manistique... "	8.00	13.50	6.50	11.50	Smith & Adams.
Manitowoc.....Wis.	11.50	20.00	10.00	18.00	L. M. & L. S. T. Co.
Marquette... Mich.	12.50	22.00	11.00	20.00	L. M. & L. S. T. Co.
" .... "	10.50	17.80	9.00	15.80	D., M. & M. R. R.
Menomonee.. "	12.00	21.50	10.50	19.50	Smith & Adams.
Milwaukee :...Wis.	11.50	20.00	10.00	18.00	L.M.&L.S.T.Co. N.M.Line.
Mullett Lake, Mich.	5.00	8.00	3.50	6.00	Inland Nav. Co.
Northport.... "	7.50	12.00	6.00	10.00	N. M. Line.
Ontonagon... "	19.50	35.00	18.00	33.00	L. M. & L. S. T. Co.
Petoskey..... "	6.00	9.00	4.50	7.00	N M Line.II,L&Co.In.Nav.Co.
" .... "	6.00	9.00	4.50	7.00	G. R. & I Ry.
Sault Ste Marie, "	8.50	13.00	7.00	11.00	L.M.& L.S.T. Co. S. & A.
Traverse City. "	7.50	12.00	6.00	10.00	Hannah, Lay & Co.

The above fares include meals and berths on the Steamers between Mackinac Island and destination. Meals and berths are extra on the steamers between Cleveland, Detroit and Mackinac Island. $3.00 or $3.50 added to the single trip rate, and $6.00 or $7.00 to the round trip rate will cover the extras from Detroit. From Cleveland, add $4.50 or $6.00 single trip, and $9.50 or $11.00 round trip.

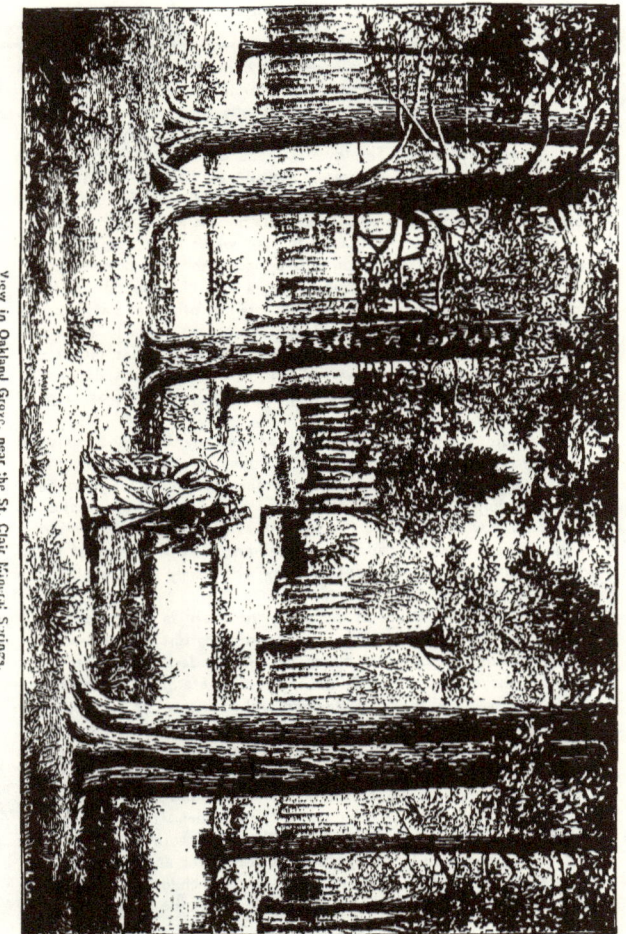

View in Oakland Grove, near the St. Clair Mineral Springs.

These floating palaces were recently built especially for the summer tourists' travel. The forward and after saloons finished in mahogany and walnut respectively are magnificently appointed and tastefully decorated, and their elegant rooms and parlors are replete with all modern improvements. The lower saloons are devoted exclusively to dining halls, thus entirely separating the culinary departments from the main saloons and sleeping apartments. This desirable feature is only possible on the large side-wheel steamers of this line. Both steamers are built of iron, and provided with four water tight compartments. Feathering paddles give them unusual speed, without jar or noise.

Visitors to the city as frequently pay a visit of inspection to these steamers as to any other attraction which the city offers, and at his office the General Passenger Agent will be found ever ready to show and explain. Courteous employees are attentive to every want, letters and telegrams are cheerfully answered, and the best accommodations reserved to those applying early, stating fully the particulars as to party to be accommodated.

The water trip thus afforded is not excelled anywhere, and the round trip affords a daylight view of all portions of the pleasant route. Occasionally parties find it agreeable to make even more than one round trip. Certainly no more comfortable place can be found outside of one's own home in which to spend the sultry days of summer, than on board of one of these splendidly appointed steamers, and the change of scene and sniff of fresh air will benefit many who vainly seek relief at the physicians' hands.

If you wish to return on the same trip there is from four to six hours at the island between the arrival and departure of your steamer, which affords a glimpse at the curiosities and wonders. Carriages are at hand for those who wish. Round trip tickets are good for the return passage at any time, by either steamer, and your stay can be prolonged as desired. These steamers leave Mackinac about every thirty-six hours. For the benefit of those who think they cannot take the time for a round trip by steamer, a circular ticket at reduced rates can be obtained which provides for a trip one way by steamer, and the other by rail.

The cost of the trip from Detroit to Mackinac Island is the least possible to insure complete comfort. Tickets, covering transportation only, can be procured from any railroad ticket agent, at $3.00 single trip, or $5.00 round trip from Detroit. Half fare for children between five and twelve years of age. Meals are 50 cents each, the same price being charged for children over three years old, under that age 25 cents, and they can be brought to the first table.

General Offices Detroit and Cleveland Steam Navigation Co., foot of Wayne Street, Detroit, Mich

D. CARTER,   **J. F. HENDERSON,**   **C. D. WHITCOMB,**
GENERAL MANAGER.   GENERAL FREIGHT AGENT,   GENERAL PASSENGER AND TICKET AGENT

The running time from Detroit includes four meals, which, at 50 cents each would be $2.00 each way. An upper berth of single width in a room is $1.00, a lower berth of double width is $1.50.

Put these items together, say for

	Single Trip.	Round Trip.
Transportation..........................	$ 3.00..	$ 5.00
4 meals at 50 cents each................	2.00..	4.00
An upper berth........................	1 00..	2.00
Total with upper berth..............	$ 6.00..	$11.00
Extra for a lower berth.................	50..	1.00
Total with lower berth..............	$ 6.50	$12.00
Or for two in one room ($6.00 and $6.50)..	$12.50	$23.00 } or $11.50
For three in one room, add transportation		} each.
and meals only for the extra person..	5.00..	9.00
Total cost from Detroit to Mackinac, for		} or $10.67
three persons occupying but one room	$17.50..	$32.00 } each.

Each room will accommodate two or three persons.

A single individual desiring to occupy a room by himself can arrange for it at an advance of the above prices.

Meals and berths are arranged for exclusively by the company.

This delightful trip to Mackinac by water, a distance of 740 miles in the round trip, occupying 2½ days, costing only $11.00 or $12.00, or about $4.00 per day, is within the reach of a large number who make a practice of leaving home for a short time during the summer months.

Parties who intend taking the Wednesday or Friday morning steamer and arrive in Detroit Tuesday or Thursday evening will be accommodated with the use of staterooms for those nights without extra charge. On arrival of the hour of departure our steamer, heading up stream springs on the stern line which throws her bow out towards the middle of the broad river, clear of all obstructions, and in a moment we are under full speed. Taking the deep channel on the east or Canadian side of Belle Isle Park our course lies E. ¼ N. for 23 minutes to a point within one mile of Belle Isle Light; then N. E. ¼ N. for 10 min. to Windmill Point Light; E. N. E. 13 min. to Light Ship; N. E. ¼ N. through Lake St. Clair 56 minutes to the Government canal. Lake St. Clair is about 22 miles long and 22 wide, the water is shallow, and large steamers leave a trail of mud behind them, thrown up from the bottom by their paddles.

40

Bird's Eye View of Canal and the St. Clair Flats (belonging to the U. S. Government) as seen from the decks of Steamers City of Mackinac and City of Cleveland.
The famous fishing and shooting grounds. Home of the black bass and duck.
Club houses, hotels and summer cottages of squatters.

ST. CLAIR FLATS, twenty-seven miles from Detroit, comprises a large area of low marshy land. There is, however, no standing water anywhere, and it is probably one of the best and most extensive fishing and shooting grounds to be found. The temperature of the pure running water is such that fish are found hard and sound even in the warmest weather. At this point the St. Clair river empties into Lake St. Clair, through six different winding channels, which form a large number of low marshy islands.

The game and fish found here attract sportsmen from all parts of the country, and it has long been famous for its fine black bass. Of the large number of pleasure seekers who patronize the river steamers, a majority stop off at this half-way place to spend the day, or enjoy a fish supper, returning by the evening steamer.

Only a few years ago there were no houses on the Flats. The river steamers stopped as they met, and transferred such passengers as desired to return to Detroit. This accommodation became very popular, but was highly inconvenient when there was much wind and sea. The fame of the place was wide spread throughout other portions of the country, before the citizens of our own city and state fairly appreciated its advantages. From an early period, however, it has been the practice of a few persons residing in Detroit and vicinity to occasionally visit the locality during the summer months for a day or two of sport, sometimes taking a scow along and rigging a shelter; but no steps were taken towards utilizing the grounds as a place of regular resort during the fishing season until the fall of 1871.

At that time a movement was made looking to the organization of a club to consist of possibly forty members, from among the young business men of Detroit, for the purpose of constructing and maintaining a club house, to be located upon lake St. Clair, at a point which might be selected as the most convenient from which to reach the fishing grounds. The proposition met with great favor, and it soon became manifest that the membership of the proposed club would exceed by far the number first intended, and that the contemplated improvements would have to be correspondingly enlarged. In the spring of 1872, the original club house was built upon its present site, about one-third of a mile above the ship canal. It was constructed entirely upon piles, with running water around and beneath it. This building has been added to and enlarged several times, and is occupied for dining purposes, and the accommodation of members' families. A capacious slip has been dredged, and the material taken therefrom utilized in the making of ground, upon which has been erected an additional building, which for general architectural appearance, and convenience of arrangement for parlor and sleeping room purposes, is truly admirable. In the rear of the first named building, and connected therewith by a covered passage way, is a two story building used as a kitchen, with sleeping apartments for servants. One of the prominent features of the Club improvements is a capacious ice-house, within which is built one of the most complete

River Bank above the St. Clair Mineral Springs.

modern refrigerator.rooms. Several additional buildings, the property of individual members of the Club, together with the long line of boat houses owned by the Club and its members, give to the place the appearance of quite a settlement. The present membership of the Club is two hundred, and is limited to that number. The organization is incorporated, and each member restricted to a single share of stock, which is in great demand, and commands ready sale at a large premium.

The location of the Club House next raised a demand for a public resort at this point ; a wharf was built about a mile further north, earth was dredged up, and Star Island created. The Star Island House was then built by the steamboat line, for the entertainment of those who desired the accommodation. This hotel has just been enlarged by its present proprietor, Mr. James Slocum, and now has a capacity for the entertainment of one hundred guests. It has a fine lawn set with flower beds and shade trees, and a good wharf. An abundance of boats, fishing tackle and all the etceteras which go to make up a perfect resort are constantly on hand. The river steamers land hundreds of Detroit citizens every day during the summer. The rates are : fare, round trip, from Detroit, 50 cents ; board at hotel, per day, $2.00 ; per week, $10.00, or 50 cents per meal ; row boats, $1.00 per day, 75 cents half a day or 25 cents per hour ; sail boats, per day, $1.50, half a day, $1.00, or 50 cents per hour ; bait, per dozen, shiners, 10 cents ; perch, 15 cents ; chubs, 35 cents ; craws, 25 cents ; frogs, 25 cents. Fishing tackle is free, or with reel, 50 cents. Guides, or punters, as they are called, can be hired for $2.00 per day. Muscalonge, pickerel, perch and black bass, the latter large and gamey, are plentiful. The fishing season commences May 1st, and lasts until October. The duck shoot-ing season begins September 1st. Decoys can be had on the island. The best class of Detroit people patronize this resort, which makes a specialty of fish suppers. A pleasanter jaunt cannot be found, and the cost is moderate. Visitors to Detroit should not miss this trip.

The North Channel Club House, which is located about one and one half miles north of this point, is reached by a small steamer every other day. Another handsome summer resort, which is to cost $30,000, is contemplated just above Star Island, on what is known as Stansell's Island.

The Flats belong to the government, and have never been sur-veyed. It is truly debatable ground, inasmuch as it belongs to no one in particular, and those who have built cottages, hotels, and club houses, hold possession by the right of Squatter Sovereignty only. The government agents at the land office say they cannot even give a pre-emption title, so that practically any one has a right to build a house anywhere on the Flats, outside of the channels.

Before many years the bank on the American side will be lined with summer cottages, club houses and resorts. The entrance to St. Clair river through the narrow winding channels at this point, was formerly attended with great danger of running aground. To improve and shorten the entrance, the U. S. Government constructed a ship canal 8,200 feet long, 200 feet wide and 16 feet deep. It was commenced in 1867, and completed in 1871, at a cost of $653,550. The banks of the canal have a fine growth of willow trees, and a light house is maintained at each end. Steamers are required to slow down to six miles per hour, in passing through, thereby preventing the wash of its sides. The steamers of this line do not stop at the Flats, the current being swift and the wharves too short to moor a long steamer securely.

Second Ward School, near St. Clair Mineral Springs.

A mile further up the channel, Joe Bedor, a French squatter and fisherman, entertains those who prefer less restraint and more common fare, than is found at the more pretentious Star Island. At the bend, on the east side is located the Canadian Club House. This property includes the entire flats on this side of the channel, and is leased from the Canadian government. The members of this club reside mostly at Toronto and Ottawa. About two miles farther on is the beautiful St. Clair river, which is 48 miles long and 1¼ wide. Some of the islands at its mouth are inhabited by a small number of Indians. Steamers keep in the middle of the river, unless they have landings to make, and tourists greatly enjoy this portion of the trip. Some six miles from its mouth on the Canada side, the Chenal-Ecarte river empties into the St. Clair. The name means the lost channel, and is pronounced by the Canadians, Sni-cart-e. Small Canadian steamers navigate this river for some miles, touching at Wallaceburg and Dresden.

MARINE CITY, 50 miles from Detroit, on St. Clair river at the mouth of Belle river, has 2,000 inhabitants. Those seeking rest from business cares would find this place both quiet and attractive, and unembarrassed by the strict social formalities so common to fashionable resorts. Comfortable hotel accommodations can be had at reasonable rates, it has all the advantages of the much and justly praised St. Clair river, is but a short distance from the hunting and fishing grounds of the St. Clair Flats, and withal it has the best of facilities for keeping informed of the doings of the outside world. No place of its size in the country has so extensively engaged in ship building, some two hundred vessels of various classes have been turned out, and a vessel may be seen under construction on the stocks at any time.

The Marine City Stave Co. recently discovered a bed of salt rock or salt in its natural state, after boring to the depth of 1,700 feet, and is now engaged in manufacturing a superior quality of the saline in large quantities, having the most extensive works in the State. The process of dissolving this rock is by pumping the St. Clair river water into the well, which washes the rock and becomes brine, it is then forced up into tanks and made back into salt. This great basin of salt, which as far as discovered is 115 feet thick, promises to make Marine City the center of a great salt producing country.

As one writer happily puts it, " The conspicuous enterprise of the Detroit and Cleveland Steam Navigation Co. in furnishing palatial steamers, famous no less for their comfort than speed is fast bringing the happiest results to the banks of the beautiful St. Clair river. They have caused a realization of the fact that the summer cottage of the tourist is here and with it bringing a desire for improvements that is fast making its shores bright ' with unnumbered shapes of new delight.' " While the wood lasted in quantities sufficient to make the article cheap, the steam craft of the lakes which were then mostly burning wood, got their supply largely from these river towns. The failure of the supply as a business accounts for so many wharves being allowed to go to ruin.

A little more than 50 years ago the first steamer was placed on this river. It was constructed from two canoes spread apart, and having a bow and stern fitted to them. Woodcock Island lies in the middle of the river, and Corunna is the Canadian town opposite.

By Steamers, from Cleveland and Detroit.

The St. Clair river is the connecting link between the great upper and lower lakes. The water that composes this river to day is the same that will be passing over Niagara Falls a few weeks hence. A pen description can scarcely do justice to this magnificent stream, which possesses a magnetic attraction such as would of itself almost draw pleasure and health seekers to its shores.

Unlike the great Mississippi, the beautiful Hudson, and other famous rivers of the world, the waters of the St. Clair are always clear, and varying in color from the deepest blue to the lightest green, according to atmospheric conditions. It is not subject to tides or freshets, the velocity of its current varying from two and one-half to three miles per hour. Not only does the traffic upon this river impress one with the vastness of the commerce of the great lakes, but its continually changing panoramic views produce an effect on the mind never to be forgotten.

Bowling Alley of Oakland House, near St. Clair Mineral Springs.

One of its widest and most picturesque points is at St. Clair, where the Michigan shore makes a grand curve, giving to the town built upon its high and sloping bank, a most commanding appearance.

The elegant steamer Mary makes a round trip daily between Algonac and Port Huron, this with the daily line from Detroit, and the City of Mackinac and City of Cleveland, give visitors to the St. Clair Mineral Springs and other places on the river, a frequent service by water.

47

ST. CLAIR, 58 miles from Detroit, with a population of 2,500, is situated on the west bank of the St. Clair river. The location is the highest and most charming natural site for a town to be found anywhere along the river or lake shores, between Lake Erie and Lake Superior.

While it is one of the oldest towns in the State, it is not old fashioned or fossil, neither is it crude and bustling. There are many fine and costly private residences, school houses, churches and other public buildings. Its social, religious and educational advantages are unusually excellent. Most of the leading religious denominations are represented and well sustained. Special mention should be made of the Somerville school, an institution for the thorough education of girls and young women.

St. Clair is especially favored in its salubrious climate, desirable temperature, and an unusually large number of bright skies and pleasant days ; fogs are of rare occurrence, while the autumn months are the glory of the year. Its comparative freedom from malaria, mosquitoes, etc., is a matter of great importance to tourists and invalids

The great attraction in this vicinity is the ST. CLAIR MINERAL SPRING. The waters of this spring, though of recent discovery, have, through the public spirited liberality of a few enterprising citizens, already become famous for their medicinal properties, and undoubtedly stand at the head of all healing waters, being endorsed by the highest medical authority, and especially recommended by physicians in the treatment of the following : Rheumatism in all its various forms ; neuralgia, gout, sciatica, paralysis, muscular contractions, nervous prostration, mental disorders, insomnia ; all diseases of the skin and blood—as scrofula, erysipelas, ulcers, etc. ; dyspepsia, indigestion, stomach disorders, malaria ; all diseases of the kidneys and liver ; diabetis, sprains, varicose veins, catarrh; ordinary colds, piles, spinal and cerebral disorders ; effects of mercurial poisoning, blood poison, etc.

THE BATH HOUSE adjoins the hotel building on the south, and is practically a part of it. It is furnished with 30 handsome bath rooms. Those set apart for gentlemen have commodious wardrobes; while a private dressing room adjoins each ladies' bath, a convenience which will be greatly appreciated, and which forms a distinctive contrast with any other bathing establishment in the country. The ladies' department

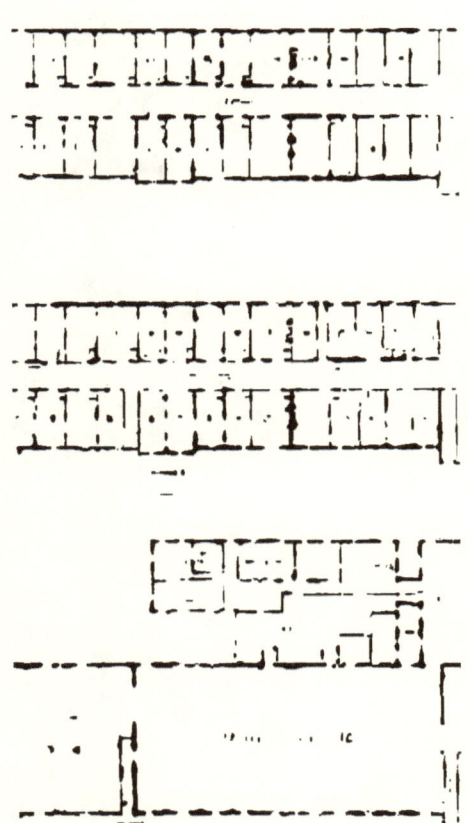

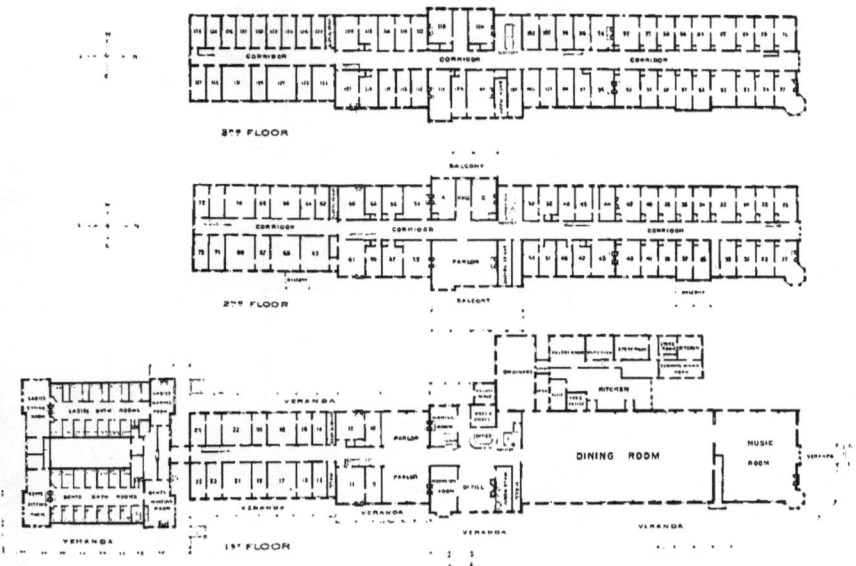

DIAGRAM OF THE BATH HOUSE AND PRINCIPAL (OR MAIN) FLOORS OF THE OAKLAND HOUSE, ST.CLAIR, MICH.

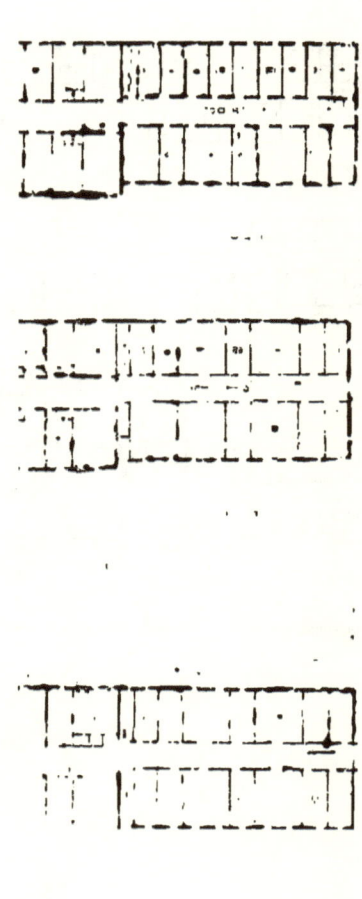

is entirely separated from the gentlemen's, each having a reception room and a parlor. The bath rooms are lighted from the roof, and heated by steam so arranged as to secure any desired temperature, and are supplied with electric call-bells, leading to the office of the attendant physician, under whose direction the baths are given. The bath tubs are porcelain lined. There are also two separate swimming baths for ladies and gentlemen respectively. Here may be enjoyed at any season the luxury of a swim in this miniature sea of tepid, diluted, ever-changing mineral water, with an equally mild and adjustable atmosphere ; where men, women and children may safely learn the so necessary art of swimming. These baths form one of the most healthful, popular and characteristic features at the Springs.

The bath house being connected with the Oakland Hotel, is an important consideration, as guests in passing between their rooms and the baths are not exposed to other than a mild and equable tempera-ture. There are also, in different parts of the bath house building, four large open fire-places, which ensure at once comfort and ventila-tion. Other internal arrangements include private consultation rooms, offices, closets, etc.

A broad and commodious veranda extends across the entire front of the bath house, and connects with that of the hotel, making a con-

Somerville School River Front, near St. Clair Mineral Springs.

49

tinuous veranda, fronting the river, 12 to 20 feet wide and 600 feet in length.

On approaching St. Clair by the steamer City of Mackinac or City of Cleveland, after having feasted your eyes for miles upon the most charming lake and river scenery, you suddenly observe a stir, and hear repeated among the passengers, " The Oakland Hotel."

Upon looking in the direction indicated, your eye is greeted with a scene which impresses you as so delightful, magnificent, restful, inviting, that you almost resolve to land, though your destination be further on. Though you may have been an extensive traveler, we venture the assertion that seldom have your eyes rested upon a group of buildings which, from a distant view, seemed so much in harmony with, so much a part of the general landscape, as " The Oakland " at St. Clair.

Reaching the hotel wharf you at once decide, if you have not already done so, to land, and with others pass from the steamer, wondering if experience will confirm your first pleasing impressions. Approaching the main building, situated a few rods distant, you observe more closely the carefully selected position, the broad and well kept grounds, its unique and attractive architecture.

As you mount the hotel steps and instinctively turn for one look toward the quiet, expanding river, you can not but admit that while Nature has been doubly kind in planting one of her most favorite springs of healing in such a favored spot, the art and hand of man have been no less successful in furthering her beneficent designs.

The hotel, in its structure, arrangements and general management, is a most admirable realization of its design, which was to combine abundant first-class hotel accommodations with charming scenery and a healthful location for those who might come to enjoy the benefits of the mineral spring, as well as for summer visitors and pleasure seekers generally.

There has already been expended upon the Oakland buildings and grounds nearly a quarter of a million of dollars, not including an extensive tract of timber land, which is being rapidly developed into a pleasure park, for the benefit of Oakland guests.

The hotel is constructed of wood, with a main frontage of 600 feet, and stands on rising ground, a few rods back from the river. Its architecture is in the general Swiss style. It is five stories high in the central portion, and surmounted by three tower-like eminences. The main part of the hotel building is a light olive-green, while the upper and tiled portion is a deep brick red, giving to the whole a decidedly novel and pleasing effect.

Along the front, on the main floor, and across the north end, are the broad verandas before alluded to ; also on the main floor in the rear, and again at the third story, front and rear—making the total length of verandas over 1,000 feet. The views from the front verandas which overlook the broad river, up and down, produce upon the beholder an effect not easily described. This grand effect is largely due to the carefully selected site, just at the right point in the river bend, and at just the right distance back, to secure the most extensive outlook in both directions. The changing moods of Nature and the floating commerce of man vary these delightful scenes, constantly adding new life and interest.

First Ward School—Catholic Church in distance, near St. Clair Mineral Springs.

The office is a handsome and commodious room, occupying the center portion of the main floor, and overlooks the river. Its most inviting feature is an immense open fire place on the north side, which, even without a fire, gives out a general feeling of home like comfort and a warm welcome. Adjoining the office is the public parlor and the usual rooms for reading, smoking, etc.

Passing southward from the public parlor along the main hall, we find opening on either side, guest rooms, furnished with rare elegance and taste, so arranged that they may be used either singly or in suites. Passing back through the office to the north

51

wing, we enter the spacious dining hall, capable of seating 300 guests. It is the frequent testimony of travelers and tourists that here is to be found one of the best supplied and best furnished public tables in the State. Adjoining the public dining hall is the ladies' ordinary, which is quite as cheerful, and the more elegant of the two.

The culinary and kitchen arrangements are on an unusually thorough and extensive scale. A glance over this department—in some sense " the heart of the house "—will at once convince you that here are exercised a thoroughness, a neatness and a system in full keeping with what you have noticed elsewhere throughout and about the Oakland.

Adjoining the office at the north we ascend the main stairway to the floors above, or, if you prefer, we will take the elevator, which is supplied with air cushions and other appliances for safety, and runs from the basement to the fifth story. On the floor above the office, in the center of the building, is an elegantly furnished private parlor, opening upon the upper veranda which overlooks the river. The remainder of this floor and those above are devoted to guests' chambers. It is frequently remarked by those who have inspected this hotel that, unlike other public resorts, the rooms—of which there are one hundred and fifty—are all uniformly pleasant and desirable

The Oakland, in short, is a model—in its location, appearance, arrangement and furnishing. The rooms are heated by steam, lighted by gas, and are connected with the office by electric call-bells.

An automatic electric fire-alarm system gives notice at the office of any fire, and indicates its precise location. Babcock fire extinguishers are placed at convenient points on each floor.

As a further protection against fire, the proprietors have lately constructed water-works, upon a plan claiming to be superior to the Holly system, having a pumping capacity of nearly two millions of gallons every twenty-four hours—capable of supplying the entire population of the city. Connected with this pump are pipes running through the various halls, to which fire hose are attached.

Surrounding the hotel are large water mains, with hydrants conveniently located, by which eight unbroken one inch streams of water can be simultaneously thrown a hundred feet high. Through this effective system an abundant supply of purest water, for drinking and culinary uses, is secured, drawn direct from the deep channel of the St. Clair river. At the north end of the hotel building, on the main floor, is a fine room, 60x40, expressly arranged and set apart as a music or concert room, dancing hall, etc. Should the Oakland guest tire of the different views, inspections, billiards, shooting gallery, bowling, and

52

other in-door games and amusements, he may regale himself with a variety of out-door pastimes and recreations.

On the lawns may be found the different games of the day.

At the boat-house you may procure a clean, dry boat, and enjoy to your heart's content, a ride on the river, or the finny tribe may lure you to their haunts with hook and line. Fish and game of all varieties usually found in this latitude are abundant here.

The river St. Clair, and the extensive St. Clair Flats have been designated by writers as the home of the black bass and duck.

For riding and driving, a fine road extends along the river, a dis-

A Drive along the Bank of the River, near the St. Clair Mineral Springs.

tance of some thirty miles. In connection with the hotel is a livery establishment, complete in all its appointments, supplying rigs of all descriptions—from the Shetland pony and cart to the stately landau, from the spirited Kentucky saddler to the spacious park wagon.

There are numerous other attractions in and about the Oakland, which you will best appreciate by a personal visit.

Courtright, the Canadian town on the opposite side of the river, is the terminus of a branch of the Michigan Central R. R. which connects at St. Thomas with the main line from Buffalo. The drive from St. Clair to Port Huron, a distance of twelve miles, is charming.

PORT HURON, 70 miles from Detroit, has 12,000 inhabitants, and is situated at the foot of Lake Huron, on the St. Clair River, the finest and purest stream of water in the world, the pride of the people who reside on its banks, and the admiration of tourists. The soil is sandy, and consequently free from malaria. The Holly Water Works supply the City with water as clear as crystal, which, with the cool breeze from Lake Huron afford two great vitalizing elements of Nature, PURE AIR AND WATER, making it a healthful City, and a pleasant place to pass a hot summer. On the opposite bank of the river (Canada) Sarnia, with 5,000 inhabitants, is beautifully situated, and has long been a great resort for Southern people. There are large hotels and all conveniences for tourists. One mile above is Sarnia Bay, a paradise for sportsmen. Splendid fishing is found here, the finest pickerel, bass and perch are caught with hook and line. There is also good shooting, and ducks of all kinds are shot in large quantities. These localities are easily reached by ferryboats. One mile above Port Huron is Fort Gratiot, where the Grand Trunk R. R. have their headquarters, and have built two of the largest Car building and Locomotive shops in this country. Over 1,000 men are employed. The Fort established in 1814 was discontinued in 1879. This place has been known for years as a fine summer resort. There are two large hotels and good boating and fishing. Two miles north of Fort Gratiot is HURONIA BEACH, a famous watering place, and great resort for families. At this point the lake narrows to the entrance of St. Clair river, and a fine view is had of the shipping passing and repassing day and night. Often fifty sail of vessels, steamers and tugs are in view at once, presenting a panorama to be greatly admired. This resort, nestled among trees, consists of a long line of cottages, with a central dining hall. A white sand beach lies between them and the lake. The buildings are all of a neat style of architecture, and present an attractive appearance. Cottagers pay for meals $4.00 per week for adults, and $3.00 for children. The dining hall is 24x154, with kitchen, ice house, laundry, pavilion, etc. The resort is established on economical principles. Servants are not allowed to accept fees of any kind. Fresh water bathing is unsurpassed. Everything is made attractive, especially for children, and it is truly called the "Children's Paradise." The cottages are also supplied with fine lake water, by hydrants in rear of each. Groves and natural forests are within the limits.

Bird's Eye View of Port Huron, Mich., as seen from the deck of Steamers City of Mackinac and City of Cleveland.

What are the great numbers of quiet, well dressed people doing here on the wharf so early Sunday morning? They are going to Sand Beach with us; they can make the round trip to-day, getting back this evening on the City of Cleveland. During the four summer months this Company sell round trip tickets every Sunday for One Dollar, and whole families avail themselves of the quiet ride. No liquors are sold on any of this company's steamers, and everything is conducted in such an orderly manner that the rowdy element is not encouraged to patronize them, hence these Sunday trips are an attractive feature of the line. Detroit people take this trip also, as they can leave home Saturday night and get back Monday morning in season for breakfast. They have about three hours at the Beach. Passengers who are destined for Goderich and the Manitoba Country leave us here and cross the river to take the Sarnia line of steamers.

The steamers City of Mackinac and City of Cleveland leave Port Huron going north four times each week, viz.: every Tuesday and Sunday morning at 7 o'clock, and Wednesday and Friday at 16 o'clock, central standard time, (which is the time on which all railroad trains are run on the American side of the river.) Passengers from the line of the Chicago & Grand Trunk R. R. and from the Saginaw Valley over the P. H. & N. W. R. R. can time it to connect with these steamers here as well as at Detroit, the fare being the same from either point, but one less meal is required.

The steamers stop at Fort Gratiot one mile above, and half way to the lake, (in the narrows of the river where the current is very swift) for passengers who have come by the Grand Trunk R. R. from Montreal and other points in Canada. These trains run on eastern standard time, which is one hour faster than ours.

The trip through the lake is a decided change from what it has been for the last six hours, and is a relief from the mental strain of seeing too much at one time. From this out all points of interest are to be seen on the port (or left hand) side, until we reach Cheboygan, the Canadian shore of the lake being too far away to be seen. We get outside, and when "abreast" of Fort Gratiot light the steamer is headed to N. $\frac{1}{4}$ W., on which course we run $3\frac{1}{2}$ hours, the outline of the shore being in sight all the way. This brings us to within 5 miles of Sand Beach, when we "haul in" to N. W. x N. for the harbor of refuge. The captain keeps well out into the lake as he likes "lots of sea room," these palatial iron steamers not being obliged to conform to the old adage "Small boats must keep near the shore."

Leaning Rock, Mackinac Island.

Main Street, Mackinac Island.

SAND BEACH, 137 miles from Detroit, is the largest village of that peninsular of Michigan, called the " Thumb," (the lower part of the State resembling a hand). The shore below is rocky, but at this point the bluffs recede, and the waters in the bay wash a beach of fine, white sand. The village is principally built on ground 40 feet above the level of the lake. The beach slopes gently back a few hundred feet, reaching a natural terrace which rises 30 feet from the lake, and back of which a few hundred feet more is a second terrace, 10 feet high, on which most of the village is built, commanding a fine view of the lake and harbor which is enclosed by a substantial breakwater built by the Government at an expense of over $1,000,000. It is 8,000 feet long, and in from 18 to 30 feet of water. The harbor contains 300 acres outside of 12 feet of water, and 160 acres outside of 18 feet of water, giving space to float a large amount of shipping. The greatest number of vessels that have at any one time sought shelter is 89. At such times the harbor is a vast forest of masts. While the harbor has proved of vast local benefit, giving unequalled shipping facilities, it is the only point on this shore where all steamers and vessels can stop.

In 1871 the town was destroyed by fire, and until 1876 it remained about as the fire left it. The village was incorporated in 1881, and has a population of 1,300. The North Star Roller Mill was the first complete roller mill built in Michigan, and has a capacity of 250 barrels of flour per day. A salt well 715 feet deep furnishes brine for manufacturing 150 barrels of salt per day.

Private capital furnished the Holly Water Works. A government life saving station established here is fully equipped with the latest and most approved apparatus. Fishing is extensively carried on; white fish, trout, bass, perch, pickerel, herring, etc., are abundant. Angling for the small fry affords capital sport, but it comes to business when white fish and trout are to be caught, and there are no finer fish in the world when taken fresh from the deep blue waters of the lake.

The Sand Beach Summer Resort Association, when in operation will afford families with hotel and cottage facilities at reasonable rates. This is a fine spot for a watering place. The harbor furnishes excellent opportunities for boating, fishing and bathing, the waters within the breakwater being always calm and safe, while the good drives,

58

Sand Beach, Mich., (Harbor of Refuge) as seen from the deck of Steamers City of Mackinac and City of Cleveland.

pleasant society and the healthful, bracing air of Lake Huron make it a most desirable place to spend a few weeks during the hot season. The great body of fresh water lying east so modifies the heat and cold that the atmosphere shows a temperature of remarkable evenness and healthfulness. The country back of this place is the only known habitat of the elk in Michigan.

The Port Huron & Northwestern trains, which will take you to the interior towns along the shore are only a short distance from the landing.

But the gong has sounded, and dinner is in order. On this latter point you have no doubt been already well informed by your inner consciousness, for the clear air of Lake Huron is an appetizer unsurpassed. Many of our fellow-passengers from Port Huron are already at the table, having no time to spare as the landing will very shortly be reached. You can even now see the outlines of the breakwater on the port bow, and the steamer will soon be headed in for the entrance.

Says a gentleman who has been a frequent passenger on these steamers : There is something very characteristic about this line, a kind of individuality that to me is admirable, and the more I see of the workings of their system for doing business, the more I am convinced that the officers on shore and on board are equally interested in a thoughtful study for the most perfect comfort of their patrons. For instance, look at this tasteful dining-room below decks occupying one water tight compartment, and the kitchen and pantry beyond, another. The iron doors between can in cases of necessity be closed by means of a lever operated from the upper deck, thus rendering either compartment water tight. Special permission was required to use these compartments connected. It will at once be seen that this arrangement relieves the upper saloons from all odors of the kitchen, noise of rattling dishes, inconvenience of cumbersome furniture, and the rushing about of numerous attendants. It requires but little observation here to realize that discipline and a strict attention to details is the key to the successful and quiet working of every department, while an excellent rule of the Company forbids any employee from soliciting fees. Dismissal from the service follows any disregard of this rule, and in fact any inattention to guests if reported to the steward receives immediate notice.

The meals, which are unsurpassed in quality and quantity, include all the luxuries of the season, and are offered at a price which barely meets the outlay. They are all served by a bill of fare equal to that of any first-class hotel.

60

Drive on the river road, below the St. Clair Mineral Springs.

STEAMER CITY OF MACKINAC.   WEDNESDAY, AUG. 15, '83.

BILL OF FARE.

DINNER.

SOUP.
Mulligatawney.   Cream of Barley, a la Royal.

FISH.
Baked White, Claret Sauce.   Fillets of Mackinac Trout, German Sauce.

COLD MEATS.
Lambs' Tongue, Pickled.   Beef Tongue.   Pressed Corned Beef.

BOILED.
Chicken, Egg Sauce.   Leg of Mutton, Caper Sauce.   Sugar Cured Ham.
Corned Beef and Cabbage.

ROAST.
Spring Lamb, Mint Sauce.   Mutton, Brown Sauce.   Turkey.
Rib of Beef, Brown Sauce.   Roast Pork, Apple Sauce.

ENTREES.
Salmi of Duck, with Olives.   Maccaroni, with Cheese.   Chicken Salad.
Mince of Veal, with Poached Eggs.   Pineapple Fritters.
Pork and Beans, Boston Style.

VEGETABLES.
Potatoes Mashed.   Green Peas.   Green Corn.   Tomatoes.
Squash.   New Beets.   Potatoes, Boiled.

RELISHES.
Sliced Tomatoes.   Chow-Chow.   Mixed Pickles.   Horse Radish.
Worcestershire Sauce.   Lettuce.   Tomato Catsup.

PASTRY.
Apple Pie.   Lemon Pie.   Whortleberry Pie.
English Plum Pudding, Spiced Brandy Sauce.

CONFECTIONERY.
Silver Cake.   Fruit Cake.   Cream Puffs.   Sponge Roll.
Maderia Wine Jelly. Vanilla Ice Cream. Strawberry Sherbet.

DESSERT.
Pecans.   Layer Raisins.   English Walnuts.   Figs.   Oranges.   Apples.

Coffee.   Tea.

MEAL HOURS.
Breakfast, 7 to 9. Dinner, 12 to 2. Tea, 6 to 8. Meals sent to
room will be charged double price.

62

River View, near the St Clair Mineral Springs.

Referring to the Company's time-table we find that the Steamers City of Mackinac and City of Cleveland leave this port, going north, Sundays and Tuesdays at 12:30 o'clock, Wednesdays and Fridays at 20:45 o'clock. Taking a course east from the wharf, a five minutes' run brings us outside of the breakwater, and we head N., N. W. for one hour until abreast of Point Au Barques light. This point is at the entrance of Saginaw Bay, through which the Saginaw, Bay City and Alpena steamers run from Saginaw and Bay City, stopping at Tawas and connecting with this line at Oscoda. This light might be called the thumb nail, as it is at the extreme end of the small peninsula called the thumb.

After passing this light, two trails of black smoke may be observed on the distant horizon. Our officers have been looking for it for some time, and recognize it at once as coming from their sister steamer the City of Cleveland. Some of our passengers who have been studying the time table have found that she was due to leave Oscoda at the same hour that we left Sand Beach, and have been expecting her along near this half-way place also; both officers and passengers are interested as the steamers approach each other. and as the two pass, indulge in an exchange of salutes of whistles, waving of handkerchiefs and shouts. Its only for an instant, both are running at a high rate of speed, and are soon far apart, then lost sight of altogether. We now follow a N. W. course for two and one-half hours, which takes us across the bay, a distance of forty-five miles. This is the only spot where we lose sight of land.

As you turn your attention once more towards the north, you may see the distant smoke of another steamer going our way ; you had not noticed her before, as she left Detroit twelve or fourteen hours ahead of us. We are fast overhauling her, and you become more and more interested as you notice how much more frequently great clouds of black smoke are thrown out from her one smoke-stack, and wonder why your fellow-passengers are again so interested. The fact of the matter is, they know the performance of these steamers so well that they fully expect them to pass everything they meet, and that, too, without any extra effort to burn more coal. The boys may pay a little more attention to the journals, keeping them well oiled and clear so she will skip along to the best advantage, but on this they are ever watchful, and we will pass her, try as she may.

But listen to the conversation; it will amuse you. On our right is a young lady from Savannah, Ga., on her first trip to Mackinac. The gentleman with whom she is speaking is her uncle from Boston, who comes up here every season.

64

" See! " she cries, " we are gaining on her! "

" Yes," says the gentleman, " we will pass her within fifteen minutes."

" Oh, my! how fast are we going ? "

" About seventeen or eighteen miles an hour."

" How fast are they? "

" Well, I don't know what steamer that is ; I should guess ten or

Fort Holmes, Mackinac Island,

twelve miles an hour. Some are that fast, and others don't make over eight miles."

" Do they carry passengers ? "

" Yes, a few. They run into small ports that this line doesn't touch, and then they get a few through passengers, because she left twelve hours ahead of us, and it was thought naturally that they would arrive at their destination as much in advance; but the fact is, we will get through first, and this steamer on her return trip will meet her again somewhere out in the lake, still working her way up slowly."

" Why, our steamer must get back to Detroit again, a long way ahead of that one ! "

" Oh, yes, she'll make two round trips while the other is making but one. In the fall when the weather is rough, the steamers of this line run in and out of their ports about on time, and sometimes leave other steamers tied up to the same wharf awaiting favorable weather, while we are making two and three trips."

" Then passengers miss it by taking any but this line? "

" Most certainly they do. When only the City of Cleveland was running on this line, it was then sometimes an object to take the first steamer, if you were not particular about comfort, but the company built this elegant City of Mackinac, and now it makes no difference how anxious you may be to get through, its better to wait for her or the City of Cleveland, whichever happens to leave first, and you'll arrive at Mackinac Island ahead, every time, and even at Alpena, practically as soon."

But here we go, past our friend, like an arrow shot from a bow, and the shouts die out, handkerchiefs disappear, and the craft becomes once more a mere speck in the blue distance.

Passengers do not scatter however, because we have now arrived abreast of the wharf at Oscoda, and the wheelsman is hard at work throwing his wheel over to starboard for a ' two mile run ' due west to the landing, which is at a sharp right angle to the course we have been following."

Among the amusing incidents which often occur on a long route like this, was one at Sand Beach not long ago. It so happened that one of the fastest one pipe steamers was just leaving the harbor going north, as the City of Cleveland was coming in at the lower entrance, bound in the same direction. The City of Cleveland was one hour and fifteen minutes discharging and taking on freight. On getting under way it was only one hour and ten minutes before she passed the first steamer at such a rapid rate that passengers thought the one

66

pipe was laying still. Shortly after a dense fog arose, but the City of Cleveland made Oscoda just the same as though it was a clear day. Without the thorough system and close watchfulness of our officers this would not be possible. As they cannot see, they are obliged to know. Some two hours later while discharging freight, this one pipe steamer came along signaling with her whistle that she could not find the entrance and asking for assistance, which the captain promptly rendered, by signals from the Cleveland's whistle.

The rough exterior of a sailor has a tender spot beneath,
And should distress be signalled, will always take a reef.

Arch Rock, Mackinac Island.

OSCODA, 195 miles from Detroit, has 2,000 inhabitants, and is located at the mouth and on the north-side of the Au Sable river. It was settled in 1874. The adjacent country comprises extensive forests of pine, and lumbering is one of its chief interests. It also has extensive salt works. The Detroit, Bay City and Alpena R. R. was completed in the fall of 1883, to Alger Station, there forming a connection with the Mackinac division of the Michigan Central R. R., making the inland towns between Bay City and Mackinac City easily accessible from this point.

The town of Au Sable is located on the south side of the river. It was settled in 1849, and has a population of 2,500. These ports have no harbor, and piers are built from the shore into deep water.

As our steamer approaches the wharf we can see that there are quite a large number of people here also. Are they all coming on board you ask? No, not all of them. The arrival of the steamers of this line always brings out the people along the shore, especially on Sundays. Quite a large number of these, however, are going with us ; some came from Harrisville, and some from Alpena this morning, at one fare for the round trip. You will find by referring to the time table again that it so happens that the City of Cleveland leaves Alpena Sunday mornings at 8 o'clock, and arrives at this place at noon, which gives about four hours here, before the City of Mackinac comes along to take them home again.

This is the only day in the week that it is possible to take a round trip for a short distance on these steamers, and you can easily imagine how delightful this arrangement must be for these people who have no extended variety of amusement. You observe again as you did at Port Huron that it is the quiet and orderly people who avail themselves of the recreation afforded.

Leaving the wharf again the steamer backs out for a quarter of a mile into the lake. The wheelsman throws his wheel over hard-a-port and heads her E., N. E. for eight minutes, or about two miles straight out from the wharf in order to clear Miller's point, and a series of shoals extending out from the main land, then throwing the wheel a starboard heads N., N. E. for one hour and ten minutes until directly opposite Harrisville, she is then headed at right angles from this course to W. x N. ¼ N. for the wharf, where we drop quite a number of our round trip passengers who came on board at Oscoda.

68

Bird's Eye View of Au Sable and Oscoda, as seen from the deck of Steamers City of Cleveland and City of Mackinac

HARRISVILLE, 213 miles from Detroit. has a population of 1,000 and is one of the flourishing villages of the west shore. The location is high, commands a fine view of the lake, and lays claim to being one of the many healthy locations of this wonderful northern Michigan. It has been visited by invalids with the most favorable results, and entertains hopes of sometime being a favorite resort.

Sixteen miles inland is Hubbard Lake, which is a beautiful sheet of water. Visitors find its scenery attractive, and in the abundance and variety of game it is the elysium of sports-men. The lake is easily reached, and has been the favorite resort of many who have keenly relished the sport and reward for their efforts, in the game that abounds in the woods and waters of the county.

Leaving the wharf again we head N. E. x E. for twelve minutes, then N., N. E. for ten minutes until abreast of Sturgeon Point Light, then north for one hour until abreast of South Point, then N. W. ¼ N. for one hour to abreast of Thunder Bay River, then N., W. ¼ W. into the river.

How long will it take to reach the wharf?

We give no time for this course, as it depends altogether on the condition of the river. The lumber kings may have been running logs down to their mills and choked it up, and some little time may be lost finding a tug to pull us in. While the city government clears up and improves the highways through town, their single, narrow highway of water is neglected, and the steam craft who serve them, unjustly suffer a heavy expense for tugs, broken wheels and loss of time.

There is a steamer close by us, she is lying still as though waiting for something. What does it mean? It is simply one of those cases where there is but little system used in the navigation of vessels, and although you can see by the moonlight that there is a broad expanse of water in the bay, still the safe channel is somewhat narrow, and unless steamers are careful to run in by a proper course every time there is a chance of getting aground. Our friend is not sure of his bearings, and is waiting to follow us in, taking advantage of our courses. You may notice this lack of confidence frequently. Four officers are constantly watching the course of our steamer, and any variation would receive their prompt attention.

Bird's Eye View of Alpena, Mich., as seen from deck of Steamers City of Mackinac and City of Cleveland.

ALPENA, a distance of 245 miles from Detroit, with 10,500 population, is situated on Thunder Bay, at the mouth of Thunder Bay river, and is the center of the lumber interests of the west shore.

On entering the river we observe a peculiarity in the construction of the wharves. Piles are driven on the water edge only, and the filling of slabs, which last a great many years, are usually covered with earth. These wharves are common to lumber sections, where slabs are made in profusion, and no salt works are at hand to use them. While the steamer is discharging freight, it will be interesting to take a short walk through the town. Here we encounter another characteristic of the lumber section in some of the streets, which are made of saw-dust.

Jonathan Birch first attempted to locate here in 1836, having found excellent facilities for building a dam at the rapids. The Indians forced him to abandon his scheme of lumbering, however, and it was twenty years before any permanent settlement was made. Lumbering commenced in 1858, and the following spring saw the first steam saw mill erected ; since then the advance has been rapid, and reflects credit on the energy, enterprise and ability which raised this city in a few years to the important position of metropolis of the Lake Huron shore.

Attention was first given to the fisheries in 1856. Nine tugs and twenty-five sail boats are now constantly employed in this enterprise. The principal grounds are at Sugar Island, Round Island, Misery Point, Partridge Point, North Point, Sulphur Island and Ossinake. The regular fishing boats remain out during the season, which lasts until the water freezes, while the run boats bring in each days catch, returning with stores and provisions. From the United States fish hatchery thirty millions of young white fish were shipped in the spring of 1883, and planted in Thunder Bay and Lakes Huron, Michigan and Superior.

An important event of early days was the arrival of the mail, carried by Indians from Bay City to the Sault, following a course around the shore with a train drawn by dogs.

In 1872, some fifteen acres of the business portion were burned, but a few months later saw handsome brick blocks in place of the frame buildings consumed. Private enterprise has furnished the city which was incorporated March 29, 1871, with the Holly water works and the Brush electric light.

72

The river is an important factor in the prosperity of the place, and Thunder Bay forms one of the best harbors along the shore. Approaching Alpena by water the view is one which, though it may disappoint the searcher for the picturesque, means to the business man energy, bustling life, and commercial prosperity. The singing saws, rattling trucks, noisy mill engines, and numberless steam and sailing vessels

Sugar Loaf, Mackinac Island.

passing in and out cannot but give to the practical observer the impression of a flourishing town; and indeed a happier combination of fertile resources and undaunted energy than is centered in this pleasant little city of the lakes would be hard to find.

Lake captains say that during heavy fogs in the day time, the song of the saws, unlike the mythical siren lays that lured sailors to destruction, often helps them to find the entrance.

Seven miles back of the city, and easily accessible is Long Lake, a pretty little spot with a hotel on its shore. Black and rock bass, pike and pickerel allure the sportsman, and make a short stay pleasant for the tourist.

Our company has been considerably reduced by the departure of many round trip passengers, and now, as preparations are going on for leaving this port, we find a new order of things. With care the steamer worked her way into the river, but it is another thing to get her out again. Between the floating logs and the crowded river, which is too narrow to admit of winding around, it becomes necessary to employ a tug that takes our line and tows us out stern first, until room enough is found to handle the steamer. The distance to Cheboygan, the next port, is 108 miles, which we will reach about 5.30 the next morning. Our course lies well out into the lake, with the shore in sight all the way, and in the day time is a most interesting trip. On parting with the tug, our steamer is headed S. E. ¾ E. for forty minutes, keeping the shore aboard three miles away, and giving the reefs of North Point, which extend out two miles from land about the same distance. Abreast of this point we steer E., N. E. twenty minutes for Thunder Bay Island Light, giving a wide berth to the shoals at the foot of the island. Many a craft has come to grief at this point, from over anxiety to turn her bow northward.

Life saving stations are located near this Light, also at Middle Island and Forty Mile Point, in Hammond's Bay, at the north, and at Sturgeon Point, Ottawa Point, Port Austin and Point Aux Barques on the south.

When abreast of the light we change to N., N. E. for five minutes to abreast of the light for the second time, when a starboard helm on a N., N. W. course for one hour, to Middle Island, clears the shoals at the foot of the island.

Off our course, six miles to the north, lies False Presque Isle, which has a fine lake, and is the summer resort of an Adrian, Mich. club.

We now steer fifty-five minutes N. W. x N., to Presque Isle Light. The bold, abrupt shore of this island admits of running close in, and thus affords a fine view of the place. Thence a course N. W. x W. ½ W. for two hours and fifty-five minutes, brings us abreast of Spectacle Reef Light, which is most romantically located. Out by itself on a small flat rock, ten miles from shore this light stands one hundred feet above the waters of the lake. It is ten miles south from Bois Blanc Island, and

74

fourteen miles from Bois Blanc Island Light. Here we run for forty minutes on a due west course to Cheboygan Light, then change W., S. W., and in four and one-half minutes are abreast of Cheboygan river. You see no entrance, and wonder how we shall find any.

> The fact is, you see,
> We'd be all at sea,
> Were it not for the captain's compass.

Suddenly the order comes, 'Starboard!' and lo! the river opens to our view. We plow our way up among lumber piles and floating logs which block the harbor at times to such an extent as to re-

Lover's Leap, Mackinac Island.

quire a tug to take us in and out, involving much delay and great expense. Propellers sometimes make things exceedingly lively, and take logs, boom and all out into the lake with them.

You ask, is there no law here that makes it a punishable offense to

obstruct a navigable stream ?   Appearances seem to indicate that there
is no such regulation.   Usually there is a harbor master to adjust such
difficulties and see that the channel is kept open ; and a city government disposed to protect all interests alike, would promptly remedy an
evil of this magnitude ; but here lumber is king, and all things must
bow to him.

An account of the course over which we are going, while serving to
locate points of interest gives an insight as well into the thoughtful
study and official watchfulness of a thoroughly well organized system.
Those who can realize how important is order and discipline to
the comfort and safety of all concerned, will see much to admire,
while there will not be wanting those who will invariably dub it red
tape.

The motto of this company, " Eternal vigilance is the price of
safety " is thoroughly comprehended and seconded by their officers.
The captain is placed on deck, and clothed by the U. S. government
with monarchical powers.   When making a landing, or leaving port, he
stands on top of the pilot house, and by turning a revolving cap can see
the compass and direct the wheelsman, while by bell pulls and speaking
tubes he reaches all parts of the steamer, and this Colossus obeys his
will almost without a word.

" He is not always in sight," did you say ?   Very true, but you can
depend upon it, he is not far away.   His room is immediately abaft of
the pilot house, and in it will be found a complete array of charts furnished by the government, with all known shoals and dangerous points
marked and explained.   A barometer to indicate the changing weather,
and a thermometer help to conclude his calculations.   If his eye is
not on the binnacle in front, or the compass within the pilot house, a
third compass stands near his desk, which is a tell-tale indicator of the
ability and watchfulness of mate and wheelsman, left apparently to
themselves.   Suspended over his bed is another compass, and if he
sleeps with one eye open, his hand is never off the tiller.

A captain's popularity should not hinge on the entertainment of his
passengers, for which he must sacrifice vigilance, which means the
speed and safety of his craft.   As Poor Richard says, " Lost time is
never found, and that which we call time enough always proves little
enough."   A successful captain should be strong of nerve, fertile of
resources, of temperate habits, and possessed of a good stock of judg-
ment and common sense.   The hurricane deck should be kept free
for the perfect exercise of his abilities, that he may have to contend
with but one idea, that of navigating his steamer.   " He that by the

plow would thrive must either hold or drive," and it is obvious that he can do neither, if he is doing something else.

The wheelsman is not the least important adjunct to the successful working of the steamer. It is his watchful eye and practiced hand that brings her on her course, then catches her as she comes and holds her within a quarter point, which is the test of his ability. Swinging from one point to another would add many miles and minutes to the trip.

From deck hands and watchmen wheelsmen come,
Having learned an even keel;
From wheelsmen come mates and captains,
How else would they know the wheel?
From wheelsman to mate, then to captain,
His courses are marked on the chart,
In learning the ropes, the wheel and to steer,
A sheer is wrong from the start.

Camping on Mullet Lake, near Cheboygan.

CHEBOYGAN, 353 miles from Detroit, and 17 miles from Mackinac Island, was first settled in 1846. It is well located at the mouth of the Cheboygan river, has extensive lumber interests, and is the leading commercial city of the straits.

Among the great natural advantages of the town are flowing wells, which being bored from twenty-five to seventy five feet, throw the pure, cold water to a height of five feet, and even higher when tubed.

Cheboygan river is the outlet of an extensive system of romantic lakes and rivers, which link together Cheboygan, Petoskey and Harbor Springs, and the Traverse Bay region.

A trip through this intricate inland route is a delightful novelty to the tourist, who can be provided with a means of transportation by the Inland Navigation Company's steamers, which are constructed especially for this purpose. On leaving the wharf a good view of the residences and business blocks of the town is obtained, and half a mile further up, the steamer is 'locked,' and lifted ten feet to the level of the river beyond. Three miles above this point, Black river empties into the Cheboygan, and is the outlet of Black lake which is twelve miles from the junction of the two rivers, and covers an area of six by four miles. Rapids in Black river, within a few miles of the lake, make its navigation by steamers impossible.

Mullet lake, a beautiful body of water, twelve miles long and from five to eight wide, whose shores are admirably adapted to camping purposes, is six miles above Cheboygan. It is full of fish, and its borders abound in game. Into it empty Pigeon, Indian and Sturgeon rivers.

Mullet Lake House, belonging to Messrs. Smith Brothers, is a handsome summer hotel, which cost $50,000. It has seventy-five large, airy rooms, elegantly furnished, and is especially attractive for families, being a paradise for children. The house opens June 20th. Steamers stop here for dinner.

Topinabee, a station on the Michigan Central Railroad, is on the opposite bank, two and one half miles away. The Northern Hay Fever Resort Association, organized in September, 1883, have located on land close by the railroad station and Pike's hotel, where there is a telegraph

78

Cheboygan, Michigan, from the decks of Detroit and Cleveland Steam Navigation Co.'s Steamers.

and post office, which, with the convenience afforded by adjacent stores, makes this a particularly desirable spot for a camp.

After leaving Mullet Lake House, the steamer enters Indian river, which some poet has likened to a " silver thread on Nature's carpet." Seven miles of beautiful river scenery and Indian River village is reached.

Burt's Lake, ten miles long and five wide, comes next. This is fed by Crooked, Maple and Sturgeon rivers, all large streams. Maple river is also the outlet of Douglass lake, which lies two miles north of Burt's lake. Crossing Burt's lake we enter upon the most interesting portion of the trip through Crooked river for seven miles. Owing to the narrow winding nature of the stream, it will seem at once impossible to go further, but by making very short turns and steering around abrupt angles, we thread the labyrinth, being able to pick evergreens from the shore on either side. This lake is five miles long, and famous for its excellent bass fishing, and the numerous delightful locations for camping out along its shores. Odin is at the head of Crooked Lake, where we bid good bye to the little steamer with regret, and take the train for Harbor Springs and Petoskey about eight miles distant.

This pleasant inland trip, from either Cheboygan or Mackinac Island, in connection with the Detroit and Cleveland Steam Navigation Company's steamers City of Mackinac and City of Cleveland is an attractive and comfortable route for tourists to and from the Northern Michigan resorts.

Passengers who do not leave the steamer at Cheboygan, but who perhaps have been amusing themselves with a stroll through the town, now hurry on board as the whistle blows the warning signal for departure. The gang plank is hauled in, and the City of Mackinac, springing on the stern line comes slowly round, and works her way out of the river to the Dummy Light, from thence with a starboard helm and a N. W. x N. course we head for Mackinac Island. There is always much to interest passengers in this short run of seventeen miles. On the port bow is seen Mackinac City, while further on to the north-west looms up on the horizon, the island of St. Helena. The many trails of smoke in the distance are from steamers passing to and from Lake Michigan.

The high lands ahead of us are called Rabbit's Back, which is a few miles north of St. Ignace, on the upper peninsula. On our starboard bow we see what seems to be one long continuous stretch' of shore, but which, as we approach, proves to be three islands, the first being Bois Blanc (Bob-low) the next Round, and the last Mackinac Island. Having run fifty minutes on the course from the Dummy, the captain is now on a sharp look-out for the flash of the Bois Blanc Island

BIRDS
Showing the
Compiled
STRAITS
Ford River
ROCK I.
MULLET LAKE HOTE

light, which being on the further side of the island can only be seen for a moment as we pass the intervening water to Round Island. On its reappearance on the other side of Round Island, you will hear the course changed to N, and Mackinac Island and village are now distinctly to be seen.

It was at this spot from the hurricane deck of the steamer which was stopped for the purpose, that our artist took the photograph of the Island, from which our engraving was made.

Indian River, near Indian village, on the Inland Route,
between Cheboygan and Petoskey

We are going in swiftly to the landing, and at the expiration of five minutes the captain sharply changes the course to N. x N. ¼ N., and the steamer with a sudden turn swings gracefully into the crescent bay, upon whose shores once dwelt the red-skinned Ottawa, and about whose island home rising three hundred feet above the clear, blue waters, still cluster the mystic halo of song, romance and legend.

MACKINAC ISLAND is the central point of the three great lakes. It knows no land breeze, hence the winds, no matter from what direction they may come, are always cool and refreshing. They no sooner cease blowing from Lake Michigan than they come from Lake Huron, and Lake Superior is never behind in the contest.

The late Dr. Drake says : " The Island is the last, and, of the whole, the most important summer resort to which we can direct the attention of the infirm or the fashionable. * * * The living streams of pure water, cooled down to the temperature of 44°, gush from the lime rock precipices, and an atmosphere never sultry or malarious, supersedes all necessity for nauseating iron, sulphur and epsom salts. As a health resort it is unsurpassed. Its cool air and pure water are just what are needed to bring back the glow of health to the faded cheek, and send the warm currents of life dancing through the system with youthful vigor."

The history of Mackinac may be divided into five periods.

The first period covers the time before the white man reached it, when the Indians made it their rendezvous.

The second embraces the early voyages of Father Marquette, his founding of the college for the education of Indian youths, in 1671; the death of the explorer, and three years afterwards the remarkable funeral procession of canoes in which his Indian converts brought back his body from its first burial place on Lake Michigan, to the little mission on the straits of Mackinac, which in life he loved so well.

The first vessel ever seen on these waters was the " Griffin," built by the explorer, La Salle, on Lake Erie in 1679.

In 1695, the third or military period begins. At that date Cadillac, who afterwards founded Detroit, established a small fort on the straits. Then came contests and skirmishes not unmingled with massacres, for the Indians enlisted on both sides, and finally the post of Mackinac, together with all the French strongholds on the lakes was surrendered to the English in September, 1761. In 1763 began the conspiracy of Pontiac, wonderful for the sagacity with which it was planned, and the vigor with which it was executed. Pontiac was the most remarkable Indian of all the lake tribes. He was a firm friend of the French, and to aid

82

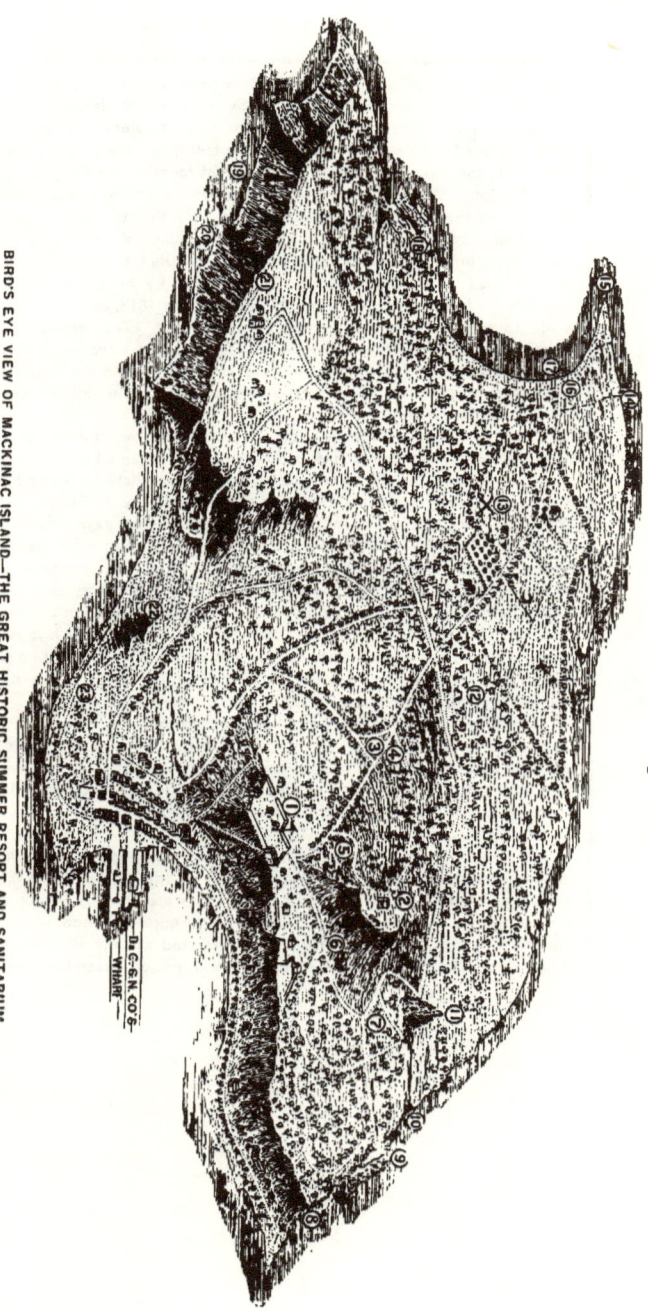

BIRD'S EYE VIEW OF MACKINAC ISLAND.—THE GREAT HISTORIC SUMMER RESORT AND SANITARIUM.

1. Fort Mackinac.	5. Skull Cave.	9. Arch Rock.	13. Battlefield 1814.	17. British Landing.	21. Pontiac's Lookout.
2. Fort Holmes.	6. Quarry 1780.	10. Ledyard's Cliffs.	14. Scott's Cave.	18. Donan's Obelisk.	22. Old Indian Burying Ground.
3. Catholic Cemetery.	7. Limekiln 1780.	11. Sugar Loaf.	15. Whitney's Point.	19. Lover's Leap.	23. Distillery 1812.
4. Military Cemetery.	8. Robinson's Folly.	12. Skull Rock.	16. Ruggles' Pillar.	20. Devil's Kitchen.	

their cause, arranged a simultaneous attack upon all the English forts in the lake country. Among those taken by surprise and destroyed was the little post on the Straits of Mackinac. No soldiers were seen in these regions for a year afterwards, when a treaty of peace having been made with the Indians, troops were again sent to raise the English flag over the fort. During the war for Independence the fort was established on its present site at Mackinac Island, and the stars and stripes, superseding the cross of St. George and the lilies of the Bourbons, waved for a time peacefully over the heights; but the war of 1812 began, and the small garrison was surprised and captured by the British. After the victory of Commodore Perry on Lake Erie in 1813, an effort was made to recapture it, which proved unsuccessful. The troops sent were insufficient in numbers, the clumsy vessels which were to support them, could do nothing against the winds and waves, and not until the conclusion of peace in 1814 was the American flag again hoisted over the Gibraltar of the lakes.

The fourth or fur trading period opened in 1809, when John Jacob Astor organized the American Fur Company with a capital of two millions, and bought out the numerous struggling associations along the straits. For forty years this company monopolized the fur trade, and Mackinac, the great central market, was the busiest and gayest post on the lakes. These were Mackinac's palmy days. Her two little streets were crowded with people, and her warehouses filled with merchandise. Mr. Astor sold out in 1834. The trade now lacked the energy and controlling influence which he had given it, and the company soon became involved. In 1848 the business was abandoned. In its best days it was one of mammoth proportions, but exists now only in history. Here also the U. S. Government made the annual Indian payments, when the neighboring tribes assembled by thousands to receive their stipend.

The fifth period is the summer resort of our modern times, which distinction is mainly owing to the facilities for reaching it recently afforded by three railroads and the steamers of the Detroit and Cleveland Steam Navigation Company, all of which center here, and for the want of which Mackinac, until within a few years, remained in a transition state.

Its original name Me-che-no-mock-e-mong, was given it by the Indians, as expressive of their surprise, when at one time at Point St. Ignace a large gathering of their people who were intently gazing at the rising sun, during the Great Manitou, or February moon, beheld the Island suddenly rise up from the water and assume its present form. From the point of observation it bore a fancied resemblance to

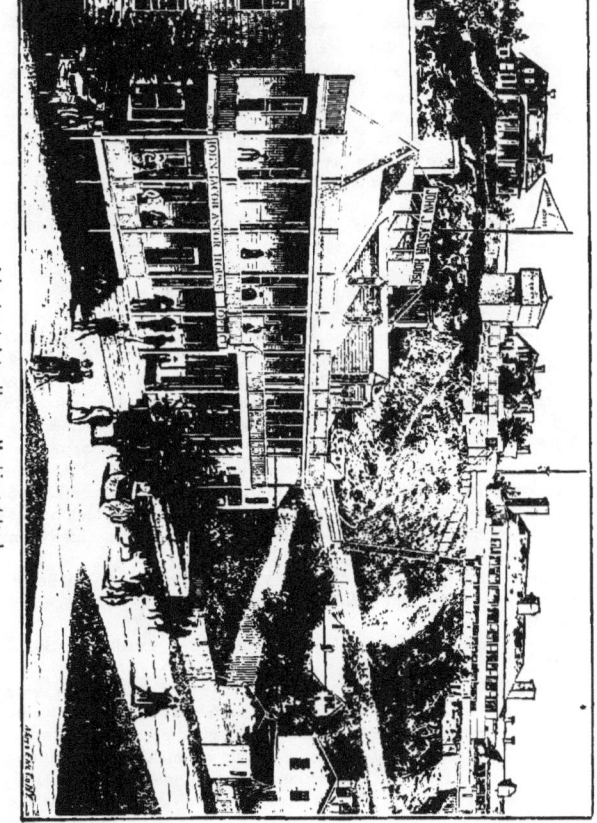

John Jacob Astor House—Mackinac Island

the back of a huge turtle, hence the name. The French called it Michilimackinac. Its present name Mackinac is pronounced Mack-i-naw.

The Indians regarded this island with a species of veneration. Tradition credits it with being the birth-place of Michabou, the Indian god of waters, and the home of the giant spirits. It is said that in passing to and fro the savages made offerings of tobacco and other articles to the Great Spirits in order to gain their good will. These deities were supposed to have a subterranean abode under the island, the entrance to which was near the base of the hill, just below the present southern gate of the fort.

The island was often the chosen home of the savage tribes, probably from the security which it afforded against their enemies.

July 15th, 1780, the British abandoned the fort at Old Mackinaw, and transferred the garrison to Mackinac Island, where they built the present Fort Mackinac The history of modern Mackinac properly begins at this date. By a treaty of peace between Great Britain and the United States, signed at Paris September 3d, 1783, the island fell within the boundary of the United States, but under various pretences the English refused to withdraw their troops. By a second treaty of amity, commerce and navigation concluded November 19, 1794, it was stipulated that the British should withdraw on or before June 1, 1796. Two companies of U. S. troops arrived October, 1796, and took possession, a previous treaty of peace with the Indians having secured from them the post.

During the war of 1812, the Island was surrendered to the British, and again restored to the United States by a treaty signed December 24, 1814.

The first steamboat to arrive at Mackinac was the Walk-in-the-Water in 1819.

Mackinac Island contains two thousand two hundred and twenty-one acres, of which the national park contains eight hundred and twenty-one acres, and the military reservation one hundred and three acres. The natural scenery is unsurpassed. Nature seems to have exhausted herself in the manifold objects of interest which meet the eye in every direction. The lover of Mother Earth will hardly grow weary of wandering through its shaded glens, and climbing over its rugged rocks, each day bringing to light some new object of beauty and interest. Every spot has some wild Indian legend attached to it, some of which the author of " Hiawatha " has put into English verse. Hiawatha is the Mena-bosho of the Algonquins, and the Island of Mackinac was considered his birth-place.

86

On the Beach at Mackinac Island.

It was visited in 1669 by that pioneer of civilization, Father Allouez, who became much interested, and left records of the Indian folk lore of the place.

Mackinac village is a perfect curiosity in itself. Situated at the foot of the bluff, upon the brow of which stands the fort, it extends for a distance of a mile around the beach. The buildings are a mixture of the modern and antique, some of which were brought from Old Mackinaw when the town and fort were removed from that point after the massacre of June 4, 1763. Many of the fences are of the original palisade style.

Schoolcraft, who visited it in 1820, says: "Nothing can exceed the beauty of this Island." It is a mass of calcareous rock rising from the bed of Lake Huron, and reaching a height of more than three hundred feet above the water. Some of its cliffs shoot up perpendicularly, and tower in pinnacles like half ruined gothic steeples. It is cavernous in some places, and in these caverns the ancient Indians were wont to place their dead. Portions of the beach are level, and well adapted to landing from boats. The harbor at the south end is a little gem. In it vessels can anchor and be sure of a holding, and around it the little, old fashioned French town nestles in primitive style, while above frowns the fort, its white walls gleaming in the sun. The whole area of the island is one labyrinth of curious glens and valleys. Old fields appear in spots which were formerly cultivated by Indians. In some of them are circles of gathered stones, as if the Druids themselves had dwelt there. The soil, though rough, is fertile. The Island was formerly covered with a dense growth of rock maples, oaks, iron wood, etc., and there are still parts of this ancient forest left, but all the southern limits exhibit a young growth. There are walks and winding paths of the most romantic character among its hills and precipices. From the eminences overlooking the lake can be seen magnificent views of almost illimitable extent.

"If the poetic muses are ever to have a new Parnassus in America they should inevitably fix on Mackinac Island. Hygeia, too, should place her temple here, for it is one of the purest, dryest, cleanest and most healthful of atmospheres."

The Island shows unmistakable evidence of the water having been two hundred and fifty feet above its present line. It is a mooted question whether the lake has fallen from its original level or the island has, from some cause, been lifted up. Springs of water clear, and cold, may be found at the base of the high cliffs and scattered through other localities.

View from the Gun Platform of Fort Mackinac.

ST. IGNACE, 377 miles from Detroit, with a population of 3,000, was founded in 1671, by Father James Marquette, and for more than a quarter of a century, was the center of interest in what was then the wilderness of Michigan. It contained a Jesuit mission and college, a garrison of two hundred soldiers, with a fine fort of pickets, and about sixty houses, forming a street in a straight line. Near by clustered Indian villages, inhabited by six or seven thousand of the savages.

At this early period the town became the western commercial metropolis, and continued to flourish until some dispute arose between Cadillac, the commander of the fort, and the Jesuits, when the former returned to France, where he received a commission to found Detroit, which he accomplished in 1701. Subsequently the town declined, and in 1706 the Jesuits became discouraged, burned their college and chapel, and returned to Quebec.

It was from St. Ignace that Father Marquette set out on the 17th day of May, 1673, in search of the Mississippi river, of which he had heard so much through the Indian tribes among whom he had labored.

To St. Ignace his bones were brought in 1677, two years after his death, at what is now Ludington, and buried in a vault in the middle of the chapel which he himself had constructed, and at whose altar he had so often served.

After the chapel was burned, the final resting place of Marquette was lost sight of until a few years ago, when the site was discovered by Father Jacker, the officiating priest, excavations bringing to light fragments of the birch bark coffin and bones, which were carefully preserved as sacred relics, and an association formed for the erection of a monument commemorative of the illustrious deeds of this humble missionary.

Two hundred and twelve years after the mission was founded, St. Ignace was incorporated. The gate city of the upper peninsula is very singularly located, extending as it does in a semi-circle around the head of East Moran Bay for a distance of three and a half miles. A fine drive stretches along the shore, and the place being almost wholly built on either side of this one street, renders the town long, with very little width.

From forty to one hundred and fifty feet back from the lake, the land rises to a height of fifty feet, forming a terrace over-looking the vast expanse of water. It is most admirably and charmingly adapted for residences, and some fine dwellings have already been erected.

Its harbor is famed for its capacity, depth, accessibility, safety and beauty, the adjacent islands forming a natural breakwater.

For a century and three quarters the town ceased to be of any importance, all interest being centered on Mackinac Island. The place has recently been given new life by the operations of the Mackinac Lumber Company at one end of the town, and by the erection of the Martel furnace at the other.

The completion of the Detroit, Mackinac & Marquette Railroad is the most important improvement. Already the amount of ore, telegraph poles, ties, etc., brought in over this new road for shipment is simply immense.

It is the northern terminus of the Detroit and Cleveland Steam Navigation Company's line of steamers, where their extensive traffic for

Lake Michigan and Lake Superior ports is distributed to railroads and steamers.

The city thrives on the furnace, lumber, fishing industries and trade with the shore and inland towns, which are fast springing up along the new Detroit, Mackinac & Marquette railroad.

Marquette's grave, the old Catholic church with its ancient painting of St. Ignace, St. Anthony's, Bear Face, Castle Rocks, Rabbit's Back and Lake Chechock are full of interest to the tourist, as is also the drive to Gros Cap, and along the winding shore from Pt. St. Ignace to St. Martin's creek, a distance of four and one half miles, embracing the water front of this young city. From the bluffs fine views may be had of the lake and surrounding attractions, viz.; the various passages through which the straits of Mackinac pour vast volumes of water into Lake Huron, Fairy Isle, the big and little St. Martin's, Round, Bois Blanc, and set on the broad bosom of the matchless water, that most unique of gems, Mackinac Island.

Visitors should not neglect the opportunity of a drive among the attractions with which the place is surrounded. Joseph Turbrett, an obliging Frenchman, will be found at the landing with a team ready for service, and any desired information regarding the place can be obtained by addressing Mr. Horatio Crain, who owns a large tract of land on the bluff, which is most eligibly located for summer cottages.

Sportsmen take great delight in following the game, which have their hiding places in the virgin forests now penetrated by the Detroit, Mackinac & Marquette railroad, and tourists find this a favorite route to Marquette and Lake Superior.

This railroad has opened up to sportsmen an almost inexhaustible field for fishing and hunting. Twelve miles from St. Ignace is Lake Brevoort, which abounds in black bass of unusual size. In the three Manistique lakes, near McMillan, bass and pickerel are found, and the numerous small streams contain brook trout in large quantities. Accommodations can be had of the farmers around the lake, or good camping places conveniently found.

There is excellent trout fishing at Au Train 30 miles from Marquette, and old Munising, on Lake Superior, furnishes excellent lake fishing, while in the numerous streams in the vicinity are found brook trout. There are good hotel accommodations at both Au Train and Munising.

Marquette is beautifully situated on a bluff overlooking Lake Superior, and has great attractions for tourists. While here visitors would be interested by a visit to the iron mines, the first of which are only a few miles away. The copper regions are reached in 10 or 12 hours.

100

hall, from which meals are furnished at very near cost. Eighty acres have been neatly laid out and platted, and lots for the erection of cottages are being sold on very advantageous terms. The secretary of the association can be addressed at Kalamazoo, Mich. Last season's improvements aggregated over $20,000, one cottage costing $3,800.

A visit to the old fort will be found interesting. There are various ways of reaching it from the village. Up the steps is probably the easiest, and the view at the top is well worth the effort. The old block houses, the officers' quarters, guard house, barracks, commissary, hospital, magazine and gun platform are all points of interest, and from the latter a magnificent view is obtained. Below are seen the government stables, blacksmith's shop and granary, and beyond the company's gardens. When built, the fort was enclosed by a stockade ten feet high, made of cedar pickets, into the tops of which were driven irons with three sharp prongs projecting. The flags of three nations have successively floated over this island, which has been the theatre of many a bloody tragedy. Powerful nations have contended for its possession, and its internal peace has been continually broken by the white man's duplicity and the red man's treachery. Its history renders it classic ground, while its wild legends people every rock and glen with spectral habitants, all combining to make Mackinac Island more interesting and attractive than any other resort to be found.

" The trip from Detroit to Mackinac by one of the steamers of the Detroit and Cleveland Steam Navigation Co., was, I confess, a thorough surprise to me," says a writer to the Congregationalist. " The City of Cleveland, in which we made our sail over this delightful route, is a large, splendidly equipped steamer. Great as is its speed, its motion is smooth and graceful as that of a swan. It is almost never either late or early."

We will refer you for further facts
To " Annals," a chronicle of acts,
About " Fort Mackinac," a mile,
Dwight H. Kelton once did write.

In the army he's lieutenant,
Thus he nailed his wooden pennant,
" Annals," " Annals," to every fence.
Take one with you in going hence;
The price is only twenty-five cents.
Should you seek they're readily found;
And with this book will cover the ground.

Mission House, Mackinac Island.

Places of interest will be readily found by reference to the bird's eye view, which shows the different locations and roads leading to them, or Starr's chariot leaves at nine in the morning to visit objects of interest. It also makes a second trip in the afternoon at two. The accommodations are sufficient for a good sized party, and the charges 50 cents for each person.

View of Traverse City, Mich.

Fort Mackinac, standing on a rocky eminence just above the town, was built by the English over ninety years ago. It is now garrisoned by a small company of U. S. troops. Starting from this spot, following the foot path along the brow of the bluff over-looking the eastern part of the town, visitors fond of natural scenery will be delighted with the grand panorama of Nature which meets the view. Nearly three-fourths of a mile from the fort at the south eastern angle of the Island is the overhanging cliff known as

Robinson's Folly. The legends connected with this cliff differ in the hands of different writers. One has it that : "Captain Robinson, a gay young English officer, and a great admirer of ladies, while strolling in the woods suddenly beheld a few rods before him, a beautiful girl, who retreated as fast as he approached, until she was finally lost sight of. Once more she appeared to him, but vanished as before. A few evenings after this, the captain was walking along the path which leads to this precipice, his thoughts still occupied with the mystery, when he again beheld the girl sitting on a large stone, apparently enjoying the magnificent scene spread out before her. Escape for her now seemed impossible. Silently he approached, a crunching of the gravel under his feet, however, betrayed his presence; she turned and their eyes met. He spoke in gentle, persuasive tones, but she made no reply, retreating towards the brink, at the same time glancing to the right and left, as if seeking a loop hole of escape. The captain shuddered at the thought of her making an unguarded step, and being dashed to pieces on the rocks below. Finally in his eagerness to capture the mysterious stranger, as well as to save her from destruction should she lose her balance, the captain sprang forward to seize her, but just as he clutched her arm, she threw herself backward into the chasm, dragging her tormentor and would-be savior with her, and both were instantly dashed on the rocks below. His body alone was found, and buried near the middle of the Island. He was long mourned by his men and brother officers, but by and by it began to be whispered that the captain had indulged too freely in the fine old French brandy that the fur traders brought up from Montreal, and the lady was a mere ignis fatuus of his excited imagination, but the mantle of charity has been thrown over the tragedy, and a romantic explanation given in its place."

Another writer says: " After the removal of the fort to the island in 1780, Captain Robinson, who then commanded the post, had a summer house built upon this cliff, which soon became a frequent resort for himself and brother officers. Pipes, cigars and wine were called into requisition, for at that time no entertainment was thought complete without them, and thus many an hour, which otherwise would have been lonely and tedious, passed pleasantly away. After a few years, by the action of the elements, a portion of the cliff, together with the house, fell to the base of the rock, which disastrous event gave rise to the name."

The brow of this cliff is 127 feet high.

A little to the north of this may be seen an immense rock, standing out boldly from the mountain side, near the base of which is a beautiful little arch known as the Giant's Stairway. This arch is well worth the trouble of a visit.

90

Robinson's Folly, Mackinac Island.

A few minutes' walk along the brow of the bluff brings you to the far famed

Arch Rock. This is a curiosity which must be seen to be appreciated. It is a magnificent natural arch, spanning a chasm of eighty feet or more in height, and forty feet in width. The opening underneath has been produced by the falling of great masses of rock, which are seen lying on the beach below. A path to the right leads to the brink of the arch, the summit of which is three feet wide and one hundred and forty-nine feet above the lake. From this dizzy height a most magnificent view presents itself. Below lies the broad expanse of Lake Huron, dotted in the distance with green gems of islands, and at the feet splashes its waves upon a pebbly beach, as if they were ever hastening at the bidding of Ariel's song: " Come unto these yellow sands." Descending through the great chasm we come upon a second arch of less majestic proportions, but equally curious and wonderful, and looking up, the mighty arch seems suspended above us in mid-air. The rains and frosts have every year made great ravages, and the rock cannot long resist their action.

Taking the road leading into the interior of the island, you soon reach

Sugar Loaf Rock The plateau upon which it stands is about one hundred and fifty feet high, while the summit of the rock is two hundred and eighty-four feet above the lake, giving an elevation of one hundred and thirty-four feet to the rock itself. The composition of this rock is the same as that of Arch Rock. Its shape is conical, and from its crevices grow a few vines and cedars. It is cavernous and somewhat crystalline, with its strata distorted in every direction. In the north side is an opening sufficient to admit several individuals. The view is very fine from the top. The curious are ever eager to known what freak of Nature placed this monstrous boulder in its isolated position, looking as though it had been thrust up through the earth like a needle through a garment. Traces of water action are seen on these two rocks, and are particular examples of denuding action, which could only have operated while near the level of a large body of water like the great lake itself. To all fond of natural curiosities these two rocks alone possess attractions sufficient to justify a visit to Mackinac Island.

Now, return to the fort and set out in another direction. Half a mile to the rear, and only a short distance to the right of the road leading to Early's farm is

Skull Rock, noted as the place in which Alexander Henry was secreted by the Chippewa chief, Wawatam, after the massacre of the British garrison at Old Mackinaw. Near the house now occupied by

Private Residences near the St. Clair Mineral Springs.

Among the outside attractions are **Hundred Islands,** (Les Cheneaux, or Snow Islands) a novel and attractive group of small islands, one hundred or more in number, lying northeast from Mackinac, nestling together in all sorts of shapes and forms. Two of the group, Marquette and La Salle, are of considerable size, while the others vary from one acre to mere fairy dots upon the water. The unique beauty of this locality will well repay a visit.

The islands are reached by a mail steamer, which, leaving Mackinac Island three times a week, stops at Prentice Bay, the easterly end of the group, where accommodations can be secured, or a sail boat or steamer can be chartered at Mackinac for further explorations.

Starting out on a trip to the Hundred Islands, the bold cliffs and rugged promontories of Mackinac Island presently give way to a distant view of the main land on the north. The deep, clear water is dotted with craft in all directions, a sunny sky of brilliant blue is overhead, and the oxygen laden breeze is truly exhilarating. On reaching the Hundred Islands, both fear and curiosity is aroused by the abrupt and curious windings for ten miles, among a labyrinth of islands and bayous, forming altogether a most delightful experience not soon to be forgotten. Shoals of fish are seen through the clear, deep water.

Sault St. Marie, on St. Mary's river, ninety miles from Mackinac Island, and within fifteen miles of Lake Superior, was the first permanent French settlement within the limits of the United States. Steamers leave Mackinac for the " Soo " regularly, also for

Manistique and other ports on the north shore of Lake Michigan. Excellent trout fishing is found in the numerous streams along the shore. Accommodations can be had of the settlers on reasonable terms. At Manistique ' The Ossawinamakee,' is an elegantly furnished hotel, first-class in every particular. The natural scenery is grand, and tourists will find the place well worth a visit. Five miles west, at Indian Lake, there is fine bass fishing and hunting, also good camping grounds. Connecting steamers leave here for Escanaba and Green Bay.

From Mackinac Island the steamer Algomah makes frequent trips to historic **Mackinaw City,** seven miles distant. A few years after the Jesuits burned their college and chapel in 1706 at St. Ignace, the post on the straits was re-established and a new fort erected, this time at Mackinac City, or Old Mackinac, as it is called in history. Little is known of the annals of this place from 1721, when it was visited by Father Charlevoix, the historian of New France, down to 1760, when, as a result of the bloody war, which terminated in Wolfe's victory at Quebec, the whole northwest passed out of French control into the hands of the English.

102

MARGARET BOYD, or " Aunt Margaret," as she is familiarly called, is a woman with a history, an Ottawa indian, born at Little Traverse 70 years ago.   She is a daughter of a right royal line of chiefs, as is evinced by the carriage of her head, the flash of her eye and the beauty and smallness of her hands and feet.   She has a fair education and speaks English perfectly, has unbounded influence over the Indians, and has done Important work in translating for the church, its books into the Ottawa language.   Her sympathies are entirely with her people, she is humiliated at their degradation, and indignant at the wrongs they suffer at the white man's hands.   In 1876, Margaret had an interview with the President in the interest of some Indian families who failed to receive from the Government, deeds for their land.   She was received with courtesy and assured that every thing should be made right.   President Grant intro- duced her to his wife and several other ladies, stum- bling badly over her long Indian name. Strangers always visit the antiquated Catholic church at Harbor Springs, founded more than 200 years ago by Marquette. If the attendant p r i e s t happens to be ab- sent Aunt Margaret may generally be found at her house near by. She will un- lock the church,give them a history of the mission, and recite the wierd Indian legends of this lovely harbor.

Margaret Boyd and Son.

107

COURSES, RUNNING TIME AND POINTS OF INTEREST FROM MACKINAC ISLAND SOUTH TO CLEVELAND.

LAKE HURON DIVISION—MACKINAC TO DETROIT.

From St. Ignace—E. S. E., 25 minutes, to Mackinac Island.

From Mackinac—S., 7 min. to range of Bois Blanc Island Light S. E. x S., 53 min. to Dummy Light, thence up the river to wharf at Cheboygan.

From Cheboygan—N. E. x N. $\frac{1}{4}$ N., 6 min. to Cheboygan Light; E. 30 min. to Spectacle Reef Light; S. E. x E. $\frac{1}{2}$ E., 2 hrs. and 35 min. to Presque Isle Light; S. E. x S, 1 hour to Middle Island; S. S. E., 50 min. to Thunder Bay Island Light; S. S. W., 6 min. to Thunder Bay Island Light second time; S. W. x W. 25 min. to North Point; N. W. $\frac{1}{2}$ W. 40 min. into Thunder Bay River to Alpena.

From Alpena—S. E. x S. $\frac{1}{2}$ S., 1 hour and 5 min. to Black River; S. $\frac{1}{2}$ E., 40 min. to Sturgeon Point Light; S. W. x S., 15 min. to abreast of wharf; W. x S. $\frac{1}{2}$ S., 5 minutes, to Harrisville.

From Harrisville—S. E., 8 min.; S. $\frac{1}{2}$ E., 30 min. to Miller's Point; S. x W. $\frac{1}{2}$ W., 20 min.; S. W. x S., 15 min. to abreast of wharf; W. x S., 5 minutes to Oscoda.

From Oscoda—E., 3 min., to clear the river; S. E. $\frac{1}{4}$ E., 2 hours and 40 minutes, to Point Aux Barques Light; S., S. E., 30 min. to abreast of Port Hope; S. x E., 30 min. to abreast of harbor of refuge; S. S. W., 8 min. to Sand Beach.

Sand Beach—E., S. E., 8 min.; S. $\frac{1}{2}$ E., 3 hours and 50 min. to abreast of St. Clair river; S. W. x S. $\frac{1}{2}$ S. 10 min., to Fort Gratiot.

St. Clair river—Steamer keeps in the middle of the stream.

From Lake St. Clair Canal—S. W. $\frac{1}{2}$ S., 53 min; to Lake St. Clair Light Ship S. W. x W. $\frac{3}{4}$ W., 13 min., to Wind Mill Pt. Light; S. W. $\frac{1}{2}$ S., 7 min., to Belle Isle Light; S. W. x W. $\frac{1}{2}$ W., 12 min., to Walkerville; S. W. x S., 13 min., abreast of Wayne St. wharf; Detroit.

LAKE ERIE DIVISION—DETROIT TO CLEVELAND.

From Michigan Central Railroad wharf, foot of Third Street. S. W. $\frac{3}{4}$ W., 4 min. to Sandwich Point; S. W. x S. 5 min. to Fort Wayne; S. W. x S. $\frac{3}{4}$ S., 16 min. to Fighting Island; S. $\frac{1}{4}$ W., $3\frac{1}{2}$ min., to Grassy Island Light; S. $\frac{1}{2}$ W., $8\frac{1}{2}$ min., to Mammy Judy Light; S. x W., $4\frac{1}{2}$ min., to Grosse Isle; S. x E., 16 min., to Lime Kiln Crossing; S. x W., 3 min., to head of Bois Blanc Island; S. $\frac{1}{2}$ E., 3 min., to Amherstburg; S., $4\frac{1}{3}$ min., to Bois Blanc Light; S. x W. $\frac{1}{2}$ W., 10 min., out of the river; S. $\frac{1}{2}$ W. 5 min.; S. x E., 5 min.; S. E. $\frac{1}{2}$ S., 2 min., to Bar Point Light Ship; S. E. x E. $\frac{1}{2}$ E., 55 min., to Colchester Light Ship; S. E. x E. $\frac{1}{2}$ E., 1 hr. and 5 min., to Point Pelee Island Light; S. E $\frac{1}{2}$ E., 25 min., to Dummy; S. E. 1 E., 3 hrs. and 25 min., to Cleveland piers; then into river, to wharf at Cleveland.

By Steamers, from Cleveland and Detroit.

JEFF, is a character well-known to the travelling public, whom he has served in many different ways as a polite and attentive servant. Having once come in contact with his bright, good-natured face, his comicalities of manner, and truly original speech, his personality is not easily forgotten. Born in Connecticut in 1829, he at an early age entered the service of the old time canal packets, between Buffalo and Rochester, where as steward, he successfully served seventy-five and one hundred passengers with the best the market afforded, out of a kitchen four by six feet.

Neither could he be out-done as a swift runner. The toot of the bowsman's horn, and cry "hard to the tow path," found him, mail bag on shoulder, ready for a leap and half mile run to the post-office. With mail changed he would reach the next landing by the time the packet arrived.

In 1849, the famous May Flower, plying between Buffalo and Detroit, attracted him, where as barber, he shaved many an innocent, bound west. In 1854, he attached himself to the new steamer Plymouth Rock, of the same line, and remained until the Michigan Central railroad introduced sleeping cars.

Jeff was the first conductor to run a Pullman' sleeping car into Detroit. He continued in the service in different parts of the country until the fame of the steamer City of Cleveland revived his love for a fast, elegant steamer. At length he was rewarded for his staunch republican

JEFF—"Last Call for Dinner."

principles, by a share in the spoils at Lansing, where he was appointed door-keeper to the House of Representatives during the winter of 1882-3.

The patrons of the steamer City of Cleveland, whether during her seasons in the Lake Superior line, or latterly, in the no less popular route to Mackinac Island, will all recall with a smile and kindly word the merry twinkle of his eye, as he announced "sour tartarians," and "the last call for dinner."

109

STEAMERS
CITY OF MACKINAC AND CITY OF CLEVELAND.
FOUR ROUND TRIPS PER WEEK.

Central Standard Time.   **GOING NORTH.**   24 O'Clock System.

Dis. from Detroit.	Dis. bet. Ports.	LEAVE	LEAVE DAYS.	O'clock.	LEAVE DAYS.	O'clock.
		Detroit........ 3½ hours.	Wednesdays Fridays.	10.00	Mondays Saturdays.	22.00
50	50	Marine City.... 45 minutes.	" "	13.30	Tuesdays Sundays	1.30
58	8	St. Clair....... 1 hour.	" "	14.20	" "	2.20
70	12	Port Huron..... 10 minutes.	" "	16.00	" "	7.00
72	2	Fort Gratiot.... 4 hrs. 10 min.	" "	16.15	" "	7.15
137	65	Sand Beach..... 3 hrs. 40 min.	" "	21.00	" "	12.00
195	58	Au Sable..... } Oscoda...... } 1hr. 15 min.	Thursdays Saturdays.	1.30	" "	16.30
213	18	Harrisville...... 2 hrs. 15 min.	" "	2.45	" "	17.45
245	32	Alpena......... 6 hrs. 45 min.	" "	7.00	" "	22.00
353	108	Cheboygan..... 1 hr.	" "	15.00	Wednesdays Mondays.	6.00
370	17	Mackinac Island. 25 minutes	" "	16.30	" "	7.30
377	7	St. Ignace. Arrive.	" "	17.00	" " Arrive	8.00

Central Standard Time   **GOING SOUTH.**   24 O'Clock System.

Dis. from St Ignace.	Dis. bet. Ports.	LEAVE.	LEAVE DAYS.	O'clock.	LEAVE DAYS.	O'clock.
		St. Ignace.. ... 25 minutes.	Thursdays Saturdays.	20.30	Wednesdays Mondays.	10.30
7	7	Mackinac Island. 1 hour.	" "	21.15	" "	11.15
24	17	Cheboygan..... 6 hrs. 30 min.	" "	22.45	" "	12.45
132	108	Alpena......... 2 hrs. 15 min.	Fridays Sundays.	8.00	" "	20.45
164	32	Harrisville...... 1 hr. 15 min.	" "	10.20	" "	23.00
182	18	Au Sable..... } Oscoda...... } 3 hrs. 40 min.	" "	12.00	Thursdays Tuesdays.	24.30
240	58	Sand Beach.... 4 hrs. 10 min.	" "	16.00	" "	4.30
307	67	Port Huron..... 3 hrs. 55 min.	" "	20.30	" "	9.30
377	70	Detroit.... Arrive	Saturdays Mondays.	1.00	" " Arrive	14.00

24 O'Clock System.—Messrs. Roehm and Wright, watchmakers of Detroit, recently showed us the dial given below as one already adopted by a leading watchmaker. It illustrates how readily time pieces can be adapted to this system. The outer row of figures denote the first twelve hours from midnight, the inner row from noon until twenty-four o'clock, or midnight. "Nothing new," was the ground recently taken by the Commissioners of Patents in denying a patent for a twenty-four hour dial. This method of measuring time dates back to Alfred the Great, who made use of candle clocks, consisting of six candles, twelve inches in length, the inches marked on each. These burned four hours each, or an inch every twenty minutes, the six candles lasting twenty-four hours. We have recently discovered that many things antique are superior to the modern, and may not this be the case in the present method of comput-

Dial Showing the 24 O'clock System.

ing time? Certainly the twenty-four o'clock system would prove a great convenience, especially to the traveling public.

There being twenty-four hours, why not have a name for each particular hour, then there would be no necessity for the "A. M." and "P. M." which often leads to errors,

and as attention is being called to this easier and more satisfactory method, it would seem strange if business men who are studying accuracy and system in everything else should not finally adopt this better system of time. On ten o'clock being given as the hour of departure of steamer or train, how often is the question asked "morning or evening," while 22 o'clock would clearly indicate the time to be within two hours of midnight. From one o'clock in the morning until twelve o'clock noon the hours are the same as ever, but after twelve o'clock noon, the hours would run thirteen, fourteen, fifteen, etc., up to twenty-four o'clock, which is midnight. Twelve deducted from the afternoon hours shows the time in the old way again.

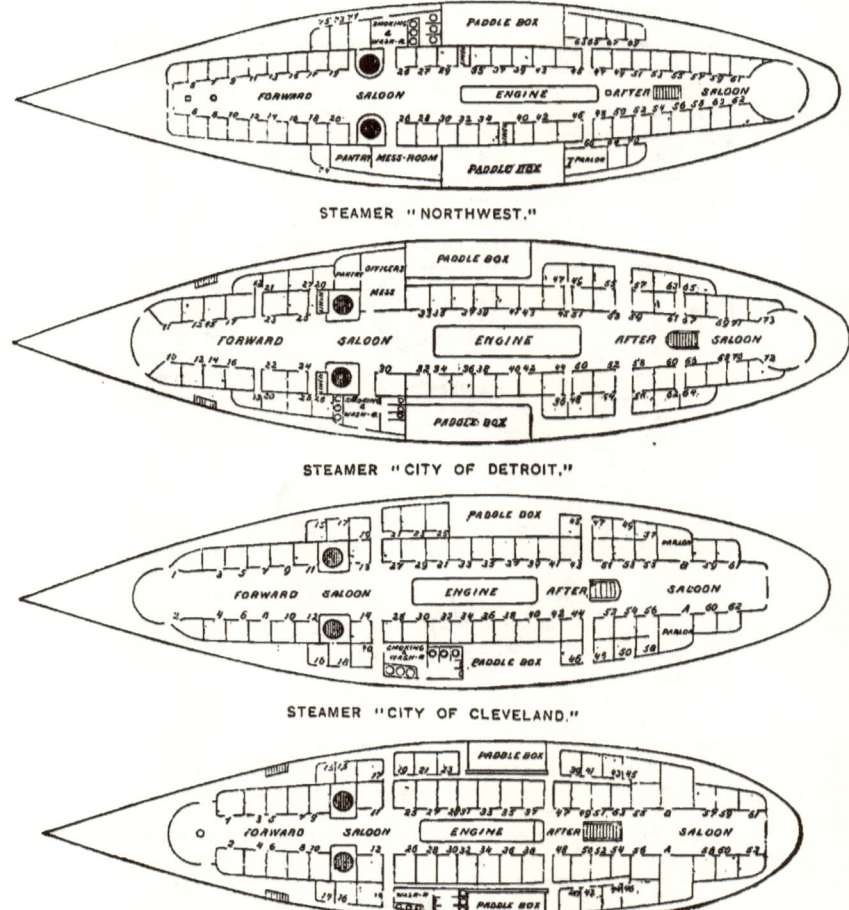

STEAMER "NORTHWEST."

STEAMER "CITY OF DETROIT."

STEAMER "CITY OF CLEVELAND."

STEAMER "CITY OF MACKINAC."

Camp of the Pittsburg Red and Gun Club, August, 1883, at One Hundred Islands, near Mackinac.

The Indians were the close friends and allies of the French, and they determined to oppose the English in taking possession of the country. All the tribes of the lake regions, under the leadership of Pontiac banded together to exterminate the English at one blow. This murderous conspiracy resulted in the total destruction of nine out of the twelve posts on the lakes, Old Mackinac being among the number.

For greater protection against these treacherous savages, the fort was removed to the Island, and Old Mackinac dropped out of sight until a few years ago, when Edgar Conklin, who at that time controlled some thirty-five thousand acres of land, which extended for twenty-five miles along the coast, surveyed a city site.

At Mackinac City, tourists can take the trains of the Grand Rapids and Indiana Railroad for Petoskey, Harbor Springs and the Traverse Bay Region. These points are also reached by water, the steamer Grand Rapids leaving from the Island. The trip through the straits towards the west is very enjoyable, and as you leave the Island you are more than ever charmed with its beauty. Seen from the straits a mile away, it is a perfect gem, and a fine subject for the artist's pencil.

Petoskey, is a charming summer resort situated on the south side of Little Traverse Bay, at the foot of high bluffs, having a water front of one and a half miles. Little Traverse Bay is nine miles long; from a width of six miles at the mouth, the shores gradually approach each other, until only two miles apart, forming the head of the bay into a half circle. The bay is here enclosed by high table lands or higher hills that approach the water in a succession of natural terraces, having the appearance of a vast amphitheatre, with an elevation of 200 feet above the bay. In the centre of this stands Petoskey, at an elevation of fifty feet. From this point the ground rises gradually to the natural limits of the town, thus giving to every one the benefits of the mild and invigorating breezes, and opening to all the beautiful views of the lake, bay and opposite shore.

Bay View, not quite two miles distant, comprising three hundred and sixty acres of land, extending for one and one-fourth miles along the beach, and one-half mile back is a resort owned by the Michigan Camp Ground Association—Methodist. A great part of the land is platted into lots, and a large number of cottages, ranging in cost from $200 to $1,000 have been built. The Bay View Hotel, and many of the cottages are supplied with clear, cold water through pipes from a never-failing spring on a hill side, seventy feet above the grounds. The natural terraces afford delightful sites for residences, and facing as they do the beautiful little bay, form a most attractive and quiet summer home.